Praise for *Where the De*

"A sensitive and searching explorat
turbulence, in the endless afterma
loss. Sequoyah's voice is powerfully singular—both wounded
and wounding—and this novel is a thrilling confirmation of
Brandon Hobson's immense gifts on the page."

—Laura van den Berg, author of *Find Me*

"A powerful testament to one young Native American's will
to survive his lonely existence. Sequoyah's community and
experience is one we all need to know, and Hobson delivers
the young man's story in a deeply profound narrative."

—KMUW Wichita Public Radio

"Dark, twisting, emotional . . . The novel holds a difficult
dialogue on intergenerational trauma, the effects of separating
children from their Nations, and the perilous outcomes if we
do not make urgent changes to the systems forcing American
Indians to assimilate and disconnect. This may be set in the
past, however, the same cycles exist today, showing that we
have not yet learned the necessary lessons to interrupt the
trauma." **—Electric Literature**

"A tender and unflinching look at shell-shocked young lives as
they try in the eddies of foster care to keep their heads above
water. Hobson writes with a humane authority but without
giving his characters any alibis."

—Brian Evenson, author of *The Open Curtain*

"I fear and ferociously admire everything Brandon Hobson creates. In this heartbreaking and vital novel there is an unconfessable world of pain, desire, and longing . . . Sequoyah, his scars, and eye makeup will leave you with wide eyes and a brimming heart." —**Chiara Barzini, author of**
Things That Happened Before the Earthquake

"Weird and intimate, like Ottessa Moshfegh's *Eileen*, *Where the Dead Sit Talking* takes us to a strange, dangerous place normally kept hidden. From the opening hook, with the unhurried authority of a master, Brandon Hobson initiates the reader into the secret lives of lost and unwanted teenagers trying to survive in an uncaring world. Creepy, sad, yet queerly thrilling."
—**Stewart O'Nan, author of** *The Speed Queen*

"Dreamlike prose . . . *Where the Dead Sit Talking* is an exploration of whether it's possible for a person to heal when all the world sees is a battlefield of scars."
—*San Diego CityBeat*

"Hobson's narrative control is stunning, carrying the reader through scenes and timelines with verbal grace and sparse detail. Far more than a mere coming-of-age story, this is a remarkable and moving novel."
—*Publishers Weekly*, **Starred Review**

"A masterly tale of life and death, hopes and fears, secrets and lies."   *—Kirkus Reviews*, **Starred Review**

"Hobson's eloquent prose and story line will keep literary and general fiction readers turning pages. Its teen protagonists offer interest for young adults."   *—Library Journal*

"[A] poignant and disturbing coming-of-age story . . . Hobson presents a painfully visceral drama about the overlooked lives of those struggling on the periphery of mainstream society."
—Booklist

"Hobson's gift to the reader is the hopeful persistence he instills in Sequoyah, despite his challenges with identity and belonging. He is a young man who is clearly scarred but thankfully not defeated."   **—Shelf Awareness**

"In *Where the Dead Sit Talking*, Hobson is once again in fine form, delivering a lyrical, somewhat brutal, and very touching coming-of-age story set in rural Oklahoma in the late 1980s. At once elegant and straightforward, poetic and cold in a way that approximates noir . . . a beautifully written novel."
—Vol. 1 Brooklyn

"Intriguing . . . Hobson has written here a dark and arresting tale."   **—Literary Hub**

WHERE
THE
DEAD
SIT
TALKING

WHERE THE DEAD SIT TALKING

Brandon Hobson

SOHO

Published by
Soho Press, Inc.
227 W 17th Street
New York, NY 10011

Parts of this novel appeared, sometimes in altered form, in
Pushcart Prize XL: Best of the Small Presses, Conjunctions, and *NOON*

Library of Congress Cataloging-in-Publication Data
Hobson, Brandon, author.
Where the dead sit talking / Brandon Hobson.

ISBN 978-1-64129-017-3
eISBN 978-1-61695-888-6

I. Title.
PS3608.O248 W48 2018 813'.6—dc23 2017029032

Interior design by Janine Agro

Printed in the United States of America

10 9 8 7 6 5 4 3 2

For Kay, Ian, and Holden

"A starving man will eat with the wolf."
—**Native American proverb**

"Poor strangers, they have so much to be afraid of."
—**Shirley Jackson**

WHERE
THE
DEAD
SIT
TALKING

I have been unhappy for many years now.

I have seen in the faces of young people walking down the street a resemblance to people who died during my childhood.

The period in my life of which I am about to tell involves a late night in the winter of 1989, when I was fifteen years old and a certain girl died in front of me. Her name was Rosemary Blackwell. It happened when she and I were living with a family in foster care, and though the details are complicated, I still think about her often. I'm alive and she's dead. I should tell you this is not a confession, nor is it a way to untangle the roots and find meaning. Rosemary is dead. People live and die. People kill themselves or they get killed. The rest of us live on, burdened by what is inescapable.

WE LEFT CHEROKEE COUNTY when I was young, and like our ancestors, my mother and I traveled out of the land with our clothes and food in sacks. We traveled through the fierce shreds of a winter storm, following a highway north into the night. We drove slowly, ice spattering the windshield. My mother talked quietly to herself, both hands on the wheel.

Maybe it was in our Cherokee blood. My great-grandfather had once traveled alone to the desert plains to meet spirits, fire and water, the two gods of hunting. He was lonely when his wife died and sought isolation, desiring a communion with nature. For food he hunted buffalo and deer, built a scaffold of poles and used it to dry fruit in the sun. He slaughtered hogs. In his solitude he was strong and worked hard, seeking the peace of his ancestors. He built fires in the night and spread ashes on his chest. He slept in the branches of bitter oaks.

My mother told me these stories about my great-grandfather while driving us to Tulsa in her El Camino. Like him, I too believed in the spirit world. Like him, I tried to see the spirits in everything around me: the trees, the open plains, the sky. I searched for them in clouds and rain. I looked into the faces of strangers and questioned whether they were messengers for me. I waited to hear their voices, as my great-grandfather had heard in his dreams. Voices that told secrets, foretold the future. Voices that brought messages. My great-grandfather claimed to have met a beautiful spirit woman. He was exhausted from traveling and welcomed the sight of her. She wore long braided hair that hung down to her breasts. She appeared to him in the desert and brought him quill baskets full of food. Her eyes were fire. She held my great-grandfather's gaze, kissed his hands, and fell into a long, deep sleep with him.

My mother and I were alone, too. My father had left us, packed up his jeep and headed west to find God. I never knew him. My mother said he joined a group of missionaries and went down to Mexico. He'd had a couple of other kids before he married my mother, but I didn't know them and it didn't matter. We never heard from him again.

I was their only child. They named me Sequoyah, meaning sparrow, after the great teacher who developed the Cherokee language. My mother said she should've named me Yellow Sky, because I was always there to bring her light, like the dawn. Back then I was too young to understand her drunkenness. When she left me alone and went out at night, I fell asleep in her bed, waking later to the noise of her coming into the room.

"Go to sleep," she told me, pulling off her boots. She collapsed onto the bed and fell asleep in her clothes. In the mornings I was there to bring her a wet washcloth and a glass of water. I was there to bring her food or medicine for her head and stomach. I never understood her sickness in the mornings back then.

"Those people you're with are poisoning your drink," I told her.

"It's normal," she said. "It's how it is for everyone."

I didn't believe her, and for a while I was afraid she was dying. What could I do? She always smelled of cigarettes and sour liquor. The nights she vomited, I was there to hold the bucket beside her bed and sing, trying to heal her. I stroked her long hair and the beads she wore around her neck. While she slept I crawled into bed beside her and hugged her until I felt numb. I didn't want her to die.

I was burned by hot grease once when I was eleven. My mother was drunk, but it was an accident. She was cooking bacon late at night and screaming at someone on the phone. I woke up and wandered into the kitchen with my shirt off, and she turned around waving the spatula. Hot grease stung my cheek and neck, burning me and knocking me down. I cried out and fell to the floor. My mother started crying and helped me into a cold shower. I remember the cold water against my skin and my mother crying and saying we should go to the emergency room, but we never did. The scars are small but noticeable enough. For a while my friends at school called me The Burned Boy.

I saw a couple of her boyfriends treat her badly. One guy kept telling her to keep her "fucking mouth shut." Another yanked her by the arm during an argument. I learned to look away, ignore them, do whatever I could to pretend they weren't abusive. These horrible men were the reason we left Cherokee County to start a new life. We rented a house just outside of Tulsa and my mother found a waitressing job but got fired for showing up drunk. The bad spirits followed us like smoke, creeping into our house and into my dreams at night. My dreamcatcher hadn't been unpacked, stored away in a box somewhere in the garage. But when I looked for it I couldn't find it. The spirits wouldn't go away. Sometimes they drifted into my bedroom and filled my head with haunting dreams. Sometimes I woke to a crashing sound, like a fist through glass.

My mother wouldn't stop drinking or staying out at night. She got waitressing jobs and then lost them. The other waitresses didn't like her. Little by little, as time passed, she grew worse until she finally landed herself in the women's prison for possession of drug paraphernalia and driving while intoxicated. She got three years since she already had a record. After that, the state took custody of me and put me in a shelter until they could find a foster home.

By fourteen, I was already smoking cigarettes and walking around alone at night. I visited my mother in prison with my social worker and kept waiting for her to straighten up like she said she would. She promised we would go back to living together again. Something inside me ached, like being held underwater and straining for breath.

At the shelter I met some friends, like Coco, who told me he pickpocketed people at the state fair. He stole toilet paper every day from the bathroom of El Vaquero until the place failed too many health inspections and closed down. For a while, before he was picked up and sent to the shelter, he slept wherever he could—in the homes of strange men, under a pavilion in a park, on the wood floors of abandoned houses. Still, at the shelter I felt confined and lonely. I saw a house fire in my dreams. The place was burning, dark smoke coiling upward into the pallid sky. In my dreams I longed to swim in that smoke, to fly around like a hawk circling in the sky. Outside, I beat on an iron fence with a spoon to drive away bad spirits. Sparks flew up and down the fence.

Nights I snuck out of the shelter and walked to the drive-in theatre. From Waterman Road to Rockland, past Pop's Grill and the El Cortez Motor Lodge where the welders and oil field workers stayed whenever they came into town for work during the oil boom. I walked to the Comet Drive-In and climbed the wooden fence that led to the gravel lot where all the cars were parked. The Comet held a special place for me. My mother used to take me to a drive-in theatre back in Cherokee County when I was little.

I liked going to the Comet when it was cool outside. I zipped up my jacket and sat on the rickety wooden bench next to kids waving green and yellow glow sticks around in the dark while their parents waited in line at the concession stand. The people around me were meaningless. They were transient spirits, shadows. I sat on the bench under a low, dark sky and got lost in the movie.

When I was little, my mother sat with me on the ground in front of the giant screen. I remember watching a western, Indians riding on horses. I remember cowboys shooting each other in dusty saloons, men playing poker and fighting. The place showed a cartoon before the movie. Once they showed the Bugs Bunny cartoon when he was shooting Indians while singing "Ten Little Indians," and even used the term "Injun." I'd seen the cartoon before and always hated it. It's one of the memories I still carry with me from those nights at the drive-in. Thinking back on it still bothers me. I wish I would've had a gun and shot the whole screen down.

I left the shelter so many times without permission they considered me a flight risk. The staff got so tired of calling the police to find me and bring me back that they told my social worker, Liz, they would stop letting me back in. But they couldn't lock me up. I just wanted to get out and walk around.

I walked around the block. I walked to the gas station and watched people go in and out. I walked across the street to the park and sat on a bench and watched younger kids play. I clapped for them when they jumped from the swings or when they climbed the monkey bars. I spit in the dirt and ground my thumb in it. Nobody paid attention.

Nights I didn't go to the drive-in theatre, I walked down to the 7-Eleven off the highway and looked at magazines, or I'd walk over to the bowling alley and talk to Leo, who was an old Vietnam vet who walked with a limp and told me stories about getting drunk and playing the mandolin in a country and western band when he lived down in Louisiana. He bought me Cherry Cokes and taught me to play chess in the snack bar one Saturday afternoon.

Liz told me if I didn't stop sneaking out she would have to make a referral as a case in need of supervision to the juvenile bureau, where they would give me a set of rules I would have to follow, and if I broke them I would have to submit to sanctions that involved spending a weekend locked up in juvenile detention. So I started trying to make things work at the shelter.

Most nights I lay in bed, listening to music on my headphones. I tried to write in a journal, but everything I wrote sounded dumb. The staff let us play the Atari after supper and watch movies when we finished our homework. At bedtime I could never fall asleep. I remember lying in the dark, staring at the dingy white curtain covering the window that overlooked the parking lot. I had a dream once that I looked out the window and saw my father standing in that parking lot. In the dream, for whatever reason, he had a beard and long brown hair. I kept knocking on the window to get his attention, but he was looking up at something in the sky. A moment later a flock of birds settled on his shoulders and head. I woke up confused.

The nights when I left the shelter no one bothered me, so I wasn't really afraid. I wore eyeliner sometimes. I'd stolen the eyeliner from a girl who was no longer at the shelter; I didn't wear it for any reason other than I liked the way it looked on me. Coco told me it went well with my dark hair.

Sometimes men tried to pick me up, but I didn't care. I kept walking. I looked so poor that I'm sure they felt sorry for me.

There was one night I met a prostitute. I'd walked past the bowling alley, over to a liquor store on McKinley Street.

The guy working there had a cat with him. The cat was silent, slinking around my legs. I picked up the cat and let it curl against my chest. The guy working there asked to see my ID and I told him I'd lost it.

"Get out of here before I call the police," he said.

The streets were quiet. I wasn't feeling well and thought maybe I should just walk back to the shelter. When I crossed McKinley, though, a woman called me over and asked me on a date. She gave me a cigarette and called me *boy* and asked me how old I was.

"Seventeen," I lied.

"Boy is seventeen," she said. She laughed.

I told her I was sick.

"Me too," she said.

She took me upstairs to a small apartment and sat next to me. I smoked one of her cigarettes and drank part of a beer, but I was feeling sick.

"It's okay, baby," she said. "You want to do something else?"

"I'm freezing," I told her.

"You just nervous," she said.

I went to the bathroom and gagged myself, trying to throw up, but I couldn't throw up. My eyes were watering when I came out. My brow was sweating and I was still cold.

When I came back to the sofa she was mashing her cigarette out in the ashtray. I sat next to her and closed my eyes. I tried to warm up.

Her stomach felt warm on my mouth. This woman, she was

nice. She had raised her shirt and put her hand on the back of my head. She pulled my mouth to her navel.

"I have to go," I said.

"What," she said. "What, what, what?"

After I left, I walked all the way back to the shelter and went straight to bed.

I QUIT TELLING MY friends at school about sneaking out late at night. None of them cared, even when I told them the story about the prostitute. Whenever Liz picked me up to take me out to eat or to a dentist appointment, we always talked about schoolwork, about staying away from drugs, those kinds of things. I smoked weed with my friend Coco sometimes, but I never did hard drugs back then. I'd seen my mom and her biker friends do cocaine plenty of times when I was younger.

Liz took me to visit my mother a couple of times when she was locked up. The guards were large men with crew cuts. They searched us when we entered and eyed me like I was someone they couldn't trust. Did they look at all kids this way? During visitation, my mother sat across from me and looked weary, her face heavy with shame and hurt.

"I'm going to make all this up to you," she told me. "You don't have to worry about no one else."

She told me she loved me and said she'd write, but I rarely received anything in the mail—usually just a short letter at Christmas or on my birthday.

The more I waited for her, the angrier I became. Soon enough I realized the less I thought about her, the better I felt.

Not long after I turned fifteen, as luck would have it, Liz told me there was a foster family who lived in the country that she thought I would get along well with. The new family I would be sent to stay with lived near Black River, in rural Oklahoma. Their house was just outside of Little Crow. In January, dead winter, Liz helped me pack all my clothes into an old suitcase my mother had bought at a yard sale. She showed me how to fold my shirts and how to pack them neatly. We left early in the morning. It was freezing outside and a light rain was falling. On the way we stopped at a diner on the outskirts of Tulsa for breakfast, one of those roadside cafés just off the interstate where travelers stop to eat. I wolfed down pancakes and sausage while Liz talked to me about respecting this family's property and their rules, otherwise I would find myself back at the shelter.

"You've grown up a lot in the past year," she told me. "I really don't need to be saying these things to you anymore. Just consider it a friendly reminder."

"Yeah," I said. "I won't do anything."

"You'll like these people. I know I've said that before, but you will."

"Are there other foster kids there?"

"Two. A seventeen-year-old girl named Rosemary and a boy who's thirteen I think. His name is George."

Liz always understood how open I was to new living

conditions. I'd been in other foster homes. At the last one, the people were nice in the beginning, but they ended up hating me, so I left. They had strict rules. They caught me smoking in their garage and yelled at me about it. They told Liz I needed to be put on probation. They made me go to bed at nine, even in the summer. I wanted to hang out with my friends and they wouldn't let me. Rules, they said. You have to follow the rules to live here. Everyone has to follow rules in life, you might as well start now. The younger kids could do whatever they wanted, but I couldn't. They hated me.

"It's fine," I said to Liz. "They can't be any worse than the last ones."

"The other thing I wanted to talk to you about," she said, "is that your mother's court hearing is next month and she could go up for parole, remember?" I could tell Liz was being gentle with me to see what my reaction would be, but I held it together. I hadn't seen my mom in two years, when Liz and another social worker took me to the women's prison to visit her. Since then she had written me a few letters, none of them saying much of anything. In one she wrote, *Dear Sequoyah, my time in here is boring. I'm trying to learn to live in this place. The food isn't great. I wish I knew something to tell you.* I wasn't even sure whether I'd kept the letters or not.

Liz told me, "Once she's released on probation I can ask the judge for supervised visitation if you want. It will come up in court."

I looked out the window at the wet parking lot. The rain

had turned to light snow, tiny flakes coming down sideways. A cluster of blackbirds scattered from a puddle and flew into the gray sky.

"I guess so," I said.

"You have time to think about it," she said. "It's a month away. I just wanted to tell you today in case you have any questions for me."

The waitress came over and took our plates and handed Liz the check. She stared at the burn marks on my face.

I've always preferred to be alone. Before my mother went to jail, I used to lock myself in my bedroom and sit by the window to avoid being around her boyfriend, Jimmy. He called me a girl whenever my mother wasn't around. He smoked Marlboro Reds and drank Budweisers that he kept in our fridge. He'd yell at my mother and accuse her of cheating, though I never saw him hit her.

One night when my mother was at work, I told him I didn't like him, and as punishment he made me go up into the attic and sit in the dark for two hours. My mother threatened to call the police, but she never did. She never did anything about it. Anytime he came over I stayed away from him. I closed the door to my room and sat at the window to watch birds outside. I always saw a line of blackbirds, grackles, along the telephone wire. They flew away into a haze of pale sky. Across the street, there was a wood-framed house where an elderly couple lived. I sometimes watched the old man mow his lawn or water the flower bed. On weekends, all day, the old woman would work in her flower bed while the husband walked around working on their house. He was always working on something it seemed, always on a ladder, repairing or painting. He carried tools around. He dragged a garden hose. That was all they ever seemed to do.

I was never completely antisocial, though I spent many days playing by myself in my room. When I was nine or ten, I had imaginary friends who weren't other children; they were small, toad-like creatures that I pretended lived in a city under water. They were blackish, oily little things with bulging eyes. They didn't so much hop as drag themselves. Some evenings they followed me home and entered my bedroom when I opened the window. When I spoke to them they listened, staring up at me with huge, watery eyes. I talked to them when I was afraid or angry or hurting. I watched them come in through the window.

Late one night in the winter I fell asleep next to the open window and ended up with a head cold. My mother brought me medicine and a wet rag for my head. I remember feeling horrible, but the cough syrup she gave me helped me sleep for hours and hours. In darkness I lost track of days and nights. At one point I woke up to see Jimmy's son, Kyle, two years younger than me, dip a small brush into a red jar and paint a doll's mouth. Later I woke to the sound of the wind knocking against my window.

"What's going to happen to us?" Kyle asked me in the dark.

"I don't know, I'm sick," I told him.

We both went quiet. My mom worked nights at the bar and had already left.

Jimmy gave me beer or whiskey some nights, which also made me sick. There were nights I couldn't open my eyes even, and there were some nights I forced myself to vomit. This night with Kyle I was really sick. I coughed until my side hurt.

"I'm sick, too," Kyle said.

I slept on and off throughout the night. In the morning I woke to sunlight coming in through the window. My mother brought me soda and aspirin. We would be moving soon.

"We still have boxes full of things," she said. "They're in the attic. You'll need to help Kyle get them down."

I closed my eyes. I wanted to be far away. Sometime later Kyle came into the room wearing a pig mask.

"I'm planning our escape," he said.

I managed to get out of bed and follow him upstairs to the attic. The room was warm and lit by a single light bulb hanging from the ceiling. He had moved things around since I'd been in there. There were only a few boxes, some tools, and an old wicker chair, where I'd once sat blindfolded.

AT THE DINER, LIZ and I were still a long way from the Troutt house. After we ate, she drove us out of the city and east along the highway. We drove past a lake, trees assembled behind it. On the radio we picked up a station that played classic country and western, Hank Williams, twangy guitars. Songs about whiskey and pain. I found it therapeutic in a strange way. We passed an oil rig and a deserted pickup truck along the side of the road. We passed billboards for churches. The churches along the highway were in old shopping centers. Church of the Covenant. Church of the Community. Church of Life. Charismatic, non-denominational churches with Bible verses on the signs out front. Billboards with Bible verses. In the distance I could see meadows and hills, fields stretching for miles.

We followed a winding road that led us past a pond and a few other houses whose owners, I imagined, were retired railroad workers and farmers living quiet, secluded lives. This was the type of life I always dreamed about living someday, being alone in a house deep in the woods somewhere. To be happy, safe. To live someplace where there was little traffic or noise or problems. To live alone, without a wife or kids.

I had to go to the bathroom, so Liz stopped at a gas station off the highway. "Ask the guy how far Little Crow is," she said. "I haven't seen any signs. We're getting close, but I want to make sure. Tell him the house is near Black River."

I went inside. The old man working at the counter was eating an egg sandwich and looking at some sort of catalogue. He wore overalls and a cap. When I asked how far Little Crow was, he made a barely perceptible sound, motioning with his head, looking past me to the highway. He stared outside as if he'd seen someone he recognized. He mumbled something in a language I'd never heard before. Maybe it was the language of rural farmers, oil field workers, charismatics. He mumbled maybe four words as he stared past me. He took another bite of his sandwich.

When I got back into the car, Liz was looking at a map. "We're getting close," she said. "What did he say?"

"I couldn't understand him."

"He didn't speak English?"

"I'm not sure."

Liz studied the map and whispered to herself. She set it between us and pulled out of the lot, gripping the steering wheel with both hands. She was getting frustrated, I could tell. I wondered whether we'd made a wrong turn somewhere that she wasn't telling me about.

We drove down a winding road, following the signs for Black River. Liz turned off the radio to help her think. This was something she did from time to time, I'd noticed—turning the radio off when she needed to concentrate on her driving. "Okay," Liz said. "This is Comanche Road."

The sun came out, if only briefly. Finally we saw the house up the road. "There it is," she said. "So much for this map, right?"

A house in the country, gleaming in the light that slanted through the trees. I saw a tall oak tree in the front yard with a tire swing hanging from it. I saw wet leaves in the yard, bushes surrounding the house. There seemed to be a large clearing in the back before an assemblage of trees. As we pulled into the drive I noticed blackbirds gathered in a tiny patch of snow. They scattered and flew into the oak tree.

Liz cut the engine and retrieved a letter from her purse. "I should give this to you now," she said. She handed me the envelope, and I recognized my mother's handwriting in cursive, all loops and swirls. I tore open the envelope and read it:

> *Dear Sequoyah,*
>
> *How are things going with you? I'm doing ok. I miss seeing your face and I wish you would come visit me. My court hearing is next month and my attorney thinks I'll be released as long as I pass U.A.s regularly. I'm gonna stay clean. I hope to see you soon.*
>
> *Love,*
> *Mom*

I decided I wouldn't think about her for now. I wondered how I was going to get this new foster family to like me. The usual thoughts raced through my mind: they knew my family history, so what did they think about my mother? My behavior? Running away from the shelter? While Liz gathered her paperwork from the back seat, I got out and heaved my suitcase from the trunk. She helped me close the trunk and smiled. "Are you ready?" she asked.

I looked at the house. Mr. Troutt, a tall man, was watching us from the front door. Standing on the porch, he was a towering presence. He was six feet tall, middle-aged, with thinning gray hair. He looked intimidating. He wore brown-framed glasses and pressed slacks. Up close, as he leaned in to shake my hand, I saw his eyes held an intense gaze.

"Harold Troutt," he said. He tried to smile but I could tell it was forced and uncomfortable. His greeting somehow made me feel he wasn't really trying to welcome me.

"We're happy you're here," he said.

"I told him the same thing in the car," Liz said. "He was worried." She turned to me. "Weren't you worried, Sequoyah?"

"A little," I said.

"Come in and meet everyone," he said, and we followed him into the living room, where he introduced us to his wife, Agnes Troutt. Agnes was a petite woman with short, light hair. She wore glasses and looked younger than Harold Troutt. I guessed she had aged better since she wasn't fully gray like he was. Her skin was beautifully wrinkled and she spoke in a quiet voice, as if she were sick, but I soon discovered she spoke like that all the time. She appeared serious and very concerned that I was comfortable, to the point that she talked to me like I was a young child.

"Sequoyah," she said, taking my hands in hers. "So nice to meet you. George is upstairs in his room and Rosemary is outside in the backyard. She spends all her time out there, sitting on the patio swing and reading books."

"They're both eccentric," Harold said. He looked at his wife. "Why don't you go find her and tell her they're here."

Mrs. Troutt was still holding my hands and looking at me,

like I was her own child returning home or something. Her eyes were almost watery.

"Agnes," Harold said.

She finally let go of my hands and excused herself. While she went to see about Rosemary, Liz and I sat on the couch across from Harold, who fumbled in his shirt pocket for a cigarette. He lit it and blew a long stream of blue smoke.

The living room had a sad plainness about it: pictures on the walls, an antique lamp, hardback books piled on the coffee table. It was a fine old house, the kind of place a grandmother might live alone. I looked at an old issue of *Life* magazine while Liz talked about getting my counseling history files to him. Soon Agnes returned and said Rosemary was sitting on the back porch but didn't want to come inside yet.

"She's moody," Harold said, looking at me. "Don't take it personally, she'll warm up to you. It takes her a while."

"She's a free spirit," Agnes added. "She isolates herself sometimes. She roams around and stays in her own world. She's very independent."

They talked about school enrollment, doctor visits, and insurance while I looked at a series of black-and-white photos in *Life* magazine of Barry Goldwater with Ronald Reagan. The Troutts prayed before meals. TV was limited to their discretion of what was appropriate. Liz assured them those rules wouldn't be a problem.

Later I walked with her to the car. She told me things would be fine as long as I respected their rules. I didn't have a choice, really. She told me how safe it was out here in the country, and that I would do well at the school as long as I remembered to follow the rules. "You'll do fine, Sequoyah. I'll call you soon. Everything will be fine."

When I went back into the house, Harold was alone in the room, still smoking. He seemed to be deep in thought. I stood there waiting for him to say something. A moment later he tapped his cigarette into the ashtray and snapped out of it. "You'll be staying with George in his room," he told me. "It's upstairs, first room on the left."

"So George is up there?" I asked.

"He is, and he knows you're coming."

I took my bag and headed upstairs, where it was warmer. I'd never stayed in a two-story house before, so I didn't mind sharing a room. When I entered, I found George sitting on the edge of the bed, writing something in a notebook. He looked up when I entered.

"Hello," I said.

He took a wadded tissue from his shirt pocket and wiped his nose. Then he came over and handed me a note before he went back and sat on his bed.

I sat on the other bed across from him and unfolded the note. It read: *I'm George.*

"I figured," I said.

I looked around the room. The walls were painted deep blue. There were drawings of fighter jets and helicopters Scotch-taped to the walls. The curtains on the windows were striped. The window by my bed overlooked the front yard and road below.

"Do you talk or just write notes?" I asked.

"I'm better at writing than speaking," he said.

"I'm Sequoyah."

He looked at the tissue in his hands. He twisted it, played with it.

"Those your drawings on the wall?" I asked him. "They're pretty good."

He shook his head.

"Maybe you can write me a note, telling me all about it."

"My friend from school gave them to me," he said. He crossed his legs and glanced at me briefly before looking away.

"So you don't talk much? That's cool with me. I'd rather you be quiet than be one of those guys who never shuts up."

He put the tissue back into his shirt pocket. I sat up and looked at him. He wouldn't look me in the eye. He kept fidgeting, staring into the floor.

"Who's better," he asked, "Bon Scott or Brian Johnson?"

"I don't know who they are."

"The singers for AC/DC," he said, "and the correct answer is Bon Scott. The albums with Bon Scott are supposedly better. It's an ongoing argument at school."

"Right," I said.

He took a pen from the nightstand and began writing something on a pad of paper. A moment later he ripped it out and brought it to me. It read:

Concerning me, I actually don't listen to much music. I just read song lyrics in the liner notes. I'm writing a novel on the typewriter downstairs. It's about a scientist living in a decaying society. The country is on the brink of destruction from an organization known as RAM. It's an acronym for "Rigid Artillery Masters." They're bombing everyone and the only survivor is a scientist who built an underground tunnel.

"Does the scientist die?" I asked.

He tapped his pen against his cheek. Then he started writing again on the pad. He ripped out the sheet and brought it to me. It read:

I don't know if he dies yet. I'm on chapter 4. I'm hoping to figure it out. I'm supposed to talk to Dr. Melig at the junior college about it. I need to do more research. In a way it's a philosophy novel.

We were silent for a while.

Finally, he spoke up:

"I keep thinking about death," he said.

MY MOTHER USED TO tell me, "Don't be quick to judge people or you'll end up getting burned." So I quickly learned to keep my mouth shut.

I gathered George was autistic or something. His whole purpose, he described in a note to me, was to stay in his room and think. To sit and think without distractions, to concentrate, to write and figure things out. When I asked what he meant, he avoided looking at me. Maybe he understood enough to know not to say anything to me. After all, I was the stranger in the house, his new roommate, a new face. I was an outsider from the street. A feral kid in black jeans. He wasn't comfortable with me yet, so I dropped it.

I turned to the window, which overlooked the front yard. Outside it was still gray and wet. There was an elm outside the window, its branches bare in the wet afternoon. A silence fell between us.

He was odd, no doubt, but there was also something delicate about him, something in the way he wrote notes, or maybe it was his long eyelashes. He was reading fairy tales mostly, he described in his note, rereading the classics, stories of wolves and children, and also science fiction stories, old copies of *Alfred Hitchcock's Mystery Magazine* that he'd found at a garage sale for a dime apiece. He was working hard on his novel.

"How do you do it all?" I asked.

"You want me to talk?"

"I'm just asking."

He sat with his head back, staring into the air, hands folded in his lap. "You like school?" he asked. "People staring at you?"

"No."

"Does it make you happy to be the center of attention?"

"No."

"Are you competitive?"

"No," I said.

"You have to empty your mind," he said. "I like to be by myself. I mean I like having something to work on all the time. My novel or reading or working on a project. What do you like to do?"

I lay back on the bed, staring up at the ceiling. "Nothing."

He whispered something to himself, and I turned to look at him. He closed his eyes and I watched him flutter his fingers in his lap. I waited for him to say something else, to ask me questions. I waited for him to dig deeper, to ask about my family, my past school, friends, anything, but he'd lost interest in the conversation. He moved his lips, whispering to himself, so I got the impression he wanted to be left alone.

A little while later I heard footsteps in the hall. Then a girl was standing in the doorway. She was slender with long, dark hair. She was wearing a green sweater, the sleeves covering her hands as she crossed her arms and leaned against the door. I thought of her as someone out of a magazine, posing in the doorway, maybe a movie star. She was really pretty. I found myself taken by the way she'd presented herself in that moment. She looked at George as if purposefully avoiding eye contact with me, but I stared at her.

The moment she looked at me, I felt the connection.

"Who are you?" she asked me.

"Sequoyah."

She looked back at George, who didn't seem to notice her. He sat cross-legged on his bed with his eyes closed. I waited for her to say something else, to ask me where I was from, where I had been living, those sorts of questions, but she didn't say anything. Maybe I found that intriguing about her, the lack of interest. The way she dismissed me the moment I said my name. The way she never smiled, not even at George's eccentricities. She glanced at me and said she was going to her room. Then she left and walked down the hall. I heard her door shut.

"That was Rosemary?" I asked George.

He spoke without opening his eyes. "Yeah, that's Rosemary."

"How old is she?"

"Seventeen," he said. "Born April twenty-third. She's a Taurus, so Harold always says she's like a stubborn bull. They make fun of astrology."

I tried to laugh, partly to get some sort of reaction from George, but he remained serious. Everyone was too serious, I thought. It was a gloomy day outside and I already wanted to leave. I looked at George, who kept his eyes closed as the room fell quiet. There was nothing left for either of us to say.

That first night, George and I sat with Harold and Agnes at the dining room table, waiting for Rosemary to come downstairs for dinner. Agnes had made spaghetti and meatballs with a salad and chocolate pudding for dessert. She filled my plate for me and asked what kind of salad dressing I liked.

"It doesn't matter," I told her.

"Do you like salad?" she asked. "It's okay if you don't like it. You don't have to eat it."

"I like it. I'm not picky."

"Liz said spaghetti is one of your favorite dishes, so I thought this would be a nice first dinner. We have ranch and Italian dressing for your salad."

"It doesn't matter. I'll eat whatever."

"How about ranch? Do you want me to pour it for you? Or you probably want to do it yourself?"

Agnes smiled at me and handed me the bottle of ranch dressing. I opened it and poured it on my salad. The spaghetti was hot and I took a bite before I realized no one else was eating.

"I don't think Rosemary is coming down," Agnes said.

Harold nodded.

"George, was she on the phone?"

George was running a finger around the rim of his glass of milk. "I don't know," he said.

"Well, I guess we'll go ahead and say grace," Agnes said. "I'll take a plate up to her."

Then Agnes started to pray aloud, during which I looked around and noticed she was the only one with her eyes closed. Harold was already putting sauce on his spaghetti, and George was pinching the fleshy part of his hand.

"Father, thank you for this food," Agnes prayed, her voice soft, "and thank you for bringing Sequoyah to our family. Help us to be a reflection of your goodness through Christ and thank you for all your blessings. Amen."

I ate head down, not saying anything.

"What do you want to do?" Agnes asked me. "I mean, when you get older? Do you know what you want to be after you finish school? George wants to be an engineer."

She smiled at me, waiting for an answer.

"I guess I don't know," I said.

"That's understandable," she said. "You have plenty of time to figure all that out."

George twisted the spaghetti on his fork.

I kept eating with my head down, but I could feel Agnes watching me. I could tell she was trying to make me feel welcome. She resembled a woman I'd met when I left my last foster home. Maybe it was the way she looked at me, a look of worry or sympathy. Or maybe it was that they were both older, attractive women in their fifties or thereabouts, with similar features. I had left my last foster home after the family caught me smoking in my bedroom. I did this from time to time, usually late at night when everyone was in bed. I'd get cigarettes from friends at school and save them. I kept them with packages of chips and cookies hidden in the closet. Sometimes I stayed out past curfew and they would call Liz, saying they weren't sure whether I was going to work out for them or not. They treated me like that, as if I were a chore barely worth the money the state paid them for taking me in. They had another foster kid, a little girl named Lacey, but she followed their rules and got along with them. She was only nine. They hated me.

One Saturday they threatened to return me to the shelter if I didn't start following their rules. They made me pick up my room and rake the leaves outside. They made me clean out the garage and sweep the porch. After all that, they told me to take out the trash and go straight to my room without coming out. I ended up in a shouting match with them, so they told me to leave. I put everything into a duffel bag, including a lighter and a book I'd stolen from the foster dad. Lacey was crying but I couldn't bring myself to tell her goodbye. I knew they wanted me gone. They called Liz and made me wait outside in the yard. It was getting dark out and I could see road dust settling from a truck that drove by. But I didn't want to go back to the shelter, so I left on my own. I jumped the fence and walked all the way to Highway 51, past the Econo Lodge and to the gas station across from it.

The woman I met there offered to take me to her home and feed me. She was old with gray hair that hung down in her face. She told me she'd been raised in an orphanage many years ago. She wore rings on every finger. When we got to her house she brought me soup on a tray and sat next to me while I ate. She wanted to put the spoon in my mouth but I wouldn't let her.

We stayed up late, drinking cheap wine and watching TV. She showed me photos of a boy with crutches. They were old black-and-white photos taken on a farm somewhere.

"His name was Arthur," she said. "He was crippled and walked with crutches until he died. He was born that way. He was only ten when he died."

I wasn't interested. She had this way of trying to laugh. She touched one of the burn marks on my face and told me my eyes were gray. Did I know they were gray? Did I want her to look into my palm and tell me my future? She reached for my hand but I pulled away. She told me a story from the Bible about a woman at a well who gave water to Jesus. The next thing I knew it was almost midnight and rain was hitting the window.

I asked her where the bathroom was and she pointed to the hall. When I got in there I didn't close the door all the way. I left it barely open. Then I lifted the toilet seat and unbuttoned my pants. I pulled out my cock and masturbated, looking at the open door the whole time until I shot into the toilet. Some of it missed the water. Some of it ran down the side of the toilet, very slowly, and I didn't bother to clean it up.

When I returned to her living room she tried asking me about my mom and family but I didn't want to talk. I told her I needed to leave.

"I understand how you must feel," she said.

"You don't understand anything," I told her.

"If you stay I'll let you sleep in the bed."

I said, "Don't you get it? I don't have to stay anywhere. I can leave if I want."

She was sitting on the edge of the divan, staring at something on the floor.

"At least wait until it stops raining," she said.

I grabbed my duffel bag. She didn't get up or try to stop me. I waited for her to say something. I waited for her to do something, anything.

Maybe all she was trying to do was help me, but I left anyway.

AFTER DINNER I UNPACKED upstairs, alone in the bedroom. I saw Rosemary briefly in the hall as I was coming out of the bedroom. She didn't seem to register my presence. She was wearing earphones, staring at her Walkman as she headed to her room. She'd been downstairs with the rest of the family.

I feared they'd been talking about me in my absence. It was a common worry, Liz always told me this. No need to be paranoid. No need to worry they won't like you. But it was hard.

Rosemary went into her bedroom and closed the door. I went downstairs to the kitchen, where Agnes was putting dishes away. The kitchen had a white enamel sink and wooden cabinets painted light blue. The wallpaper was light blue with pictures of small baskets of vegetables and fruit. The room gave off a country kitchen feel. It was a reminder I was in a rural area, a few miles outside of town. I'd never lived in the country before, so looking out the kitchen window at night was like looking in a mirror—there was vast darkness as far as you could see without any porch lights on.

When I entered the kitchen, Agnes smiled and said, "I'm glad you're here. I was about to head upstairs to talk to you. Can I get you anything?"

"No, I'm fine."

"Are you sure? Anything you need?"

"I'm fine."

"Good," she said. She wiped her hands with a dish towel. "I don't want you to think we're inconvenienced by having you here with us. We want to get to know you better. Liz said very pleasant things about you, and I want you to know you can talk to me or Harold about anything you want."

"I know," I said.

"Harold tends to spend a lot of time downstairs in the basement. Don't worry about bothering him. He does it to keep himself occupied. He keeps to himself, but I think you'll find him quite likable. Did you get a chance to talk to Rosemary?"

"Not really."

"She's an artist. She loves to draw and paint. Tomorrow she'll drive you and George to school. George will show you where to go. Liz said you're enrolled. Do you have your schedule? Do you know what teachers you have?"

"I don't know," I said. "It's fine. I've done it before."

"All right," she said. "I'm here for you, okay? Will you remember that?" She kept looking at me, waiting for me to say something, but all I could wonder was whether she was lying or not.

Looking back, I realize I wanted more than anything else to be liked, accepted. Moving from place to place, from shelter to foster home, almost always took its toll, and at fifteen I'd never gotten over the crippling anxiety of sleeping in a new room, a new bed, living in a whole new environment. While the shelter was confining and supposed to be a short-term placement, I'd grown to appreciate having my own room and how easy it was to manipulate the staff and sneak away at night. Foster homes were different. Foster homes were real families in real houses with burglar alarms and neighborhood watch groups. A teenager couldn't walk around in such a neighborhood late at night and get away with it.

Agnes and Harold told me how proud they were of George's donations and participation in the annual Walk-a-Thon for Leukemia, as well as his time spent volunteering at the local animal shelter and public library, and that they thought other students should be as passionate and proactive about such issues as he was. Over the past summer he'd done even more. His picture was in the newspaper for collecting used athletic shoes for the Perpetual Prosperity Pumps Foundation that raised awareness of poverty in Ghana or somewhere. Agnes was quoted in the paper as saying, "George has such a big heart."

"We're proud of Rosemary's accomplishments, too," she added, but didn't mention any of them.

The first night was strange. It came upon me like burning memory, how shadows spread across the wall in this new room, and in trying to sleep I revisited all the other rooms where I had slept in my past:

My room at the shelter, with its dull, concrete walls, absent of life and color, with one small window facing the brick building next door.

My room in our first house, a small house built of rock that sat near a hill in the woods in Steely Hollow, with the bedroom full of wallpaper of ships at sea, and the small closet I feared held the monsters that lived there—creatures that crawled up from the dirt below the house, who howled in the night, whose shadows cast jagged shards of light across the ceiling when I tried to sleep.

My room in the small apartment above the dirty bookstore, where I slept with a blanket the spirits had blessed with protection. I was more afraid there than anywhere. I heard sirens and traffic sounds at night. There were voices from the street outside. The room was the smallest room I've ever seen, as I now recall, and my mother's footsteps on the hardwood floors kept me awake until late in the night.

My room in the foster home after my mother was locked up the first time, a room I shared with two other boys who slept in bunk beds. I slept on a trundle bed against the wall across from the window. The room was never frightening like some of the other rooms, though the boy on the top bunk thought it was, and spent many nights crying himself to sleep.

And into this new room I was now thrown, or so it seemed, trying to sleep again, this room with its clock ticking on the wall by the door, with its shadows and lights stretching across the wall and ceiling. And I remember how, that first night in bed, I could hear George making sounds of explosions and gunfire with his mouth. It was something a younger boy might do while playing army. In the darkness I stared at the ceiling and waited for him to stop. After it went on a while I finally sat up in bed and looked over at him.

"I'm trying to sleep," I said.

"I forgot you were here," he said.

"I'm right here."

I lay in the bed with my arm over my eyes, trying to go to sleep. I felt a sadness but also a kind of confusion. There was nothing I was afraid of, and nothing to look forward to, which made me want to leave. I was like a cat in the night—that's what Liz always said. I needed a place to feel comfortable.

George turned on the lamp beside his bed and wrote something down in a notebook. He brought it to me. It read:

Sometimes I sleepwalk.

"Whatever," I said. "Just don't wake me up if you do."

He took the notebook from me and wrote something else: *If I sleepwalk I might get in bed with you, okay?*

That night I didn't sleep well. I kept waking up disoriented, confused in the darkness. At one point I got up to go to the bathroom. I didn't know what time it was, but the house was silent. As I stepped into the hall I noticed Rosemary's door was open. I walked past her room and saw her sitting cross-legged on her bed, a pillow in her lap. It took a moment in the darkness for me to notice she was looking at me. Neither of us said anything. I saw only her, sitting alone in the dark, looking at me. I walked down the hall to the bathroom. When I came out, her bedroom door was closed.

The next morning I dressed and ate breakfast with George downstairs while Rosemary got ready in the upstairs bathroom. With the dizzy smell of coffee brewing and hot oatmeal, George showed me the cassette tapes in his backpack. The tapes were Rosemary's, Agnes explained, but instead of listening to them George liked reading the liner notes, memorizing the names of band members. He could name the band's members and history without ever having listened to their music.

"The Sugarcubes," he said. "From Iceland. Do you know them?"

"No."

"Wall of Voodoo? The Smiths?"

"No."

"Morbid Opera? What about Throbbing Gristle or The

Plasmatics? Teenage Jesus and the Jerks? Who else. Boomtown
Rats, Bow Wow Wow? Castration Squad? The Raincoats?"

"No."

"I like to memorize band names," he said. "But not the
music. Never the music. Rosemary gives me the inserts of her
tapes and I read the liner notes. She listens to them."

Agnes asked if we wanted more orange juice. "You better
hurry and leave," she said, and looked at George. "Where's
Rosemary?"

He shrugged.

Agnes stepped out of the room. We heard her call for Rosemary from the bottom of the stairs. When Rosemary finally
came downstairs she walked into the kitchen and grabbed a
Diet Coke from the fridge. "I can't eat anything this early,"
she told us, as if we'd asked her about breakfast. She opened
the can and looked at us. "You guys ready?"

We took the Pontiac Grand Am out of the country and
onto the highway. George wanted to ride in back. I sat up
front next to Rosemary. She was wearing a black coat and
light blue gloves. Her hair was long and I could smell her
perfume. She played a cassette and turned it up. The music
was full of keyboards and drums. She sang along as we sped
down the highway. When we reached the junior high school,
she stopped at the corner to let George out.

He took forever checking his backpack before opening
the door.

"See you later," Rosemary said to him.

As we pulled away, she turned down the music and drove toward the high school a few blocks away.

"I have to go to the office to get my schedule," I said.

"You're a freshman, right?"

"Yeah. You're a senior?"

"I'm basically done. I have like one class I'm finishing."

She pulled in front of the high school, next to the curb. "The office is on the first floor," she said. "You'll do fine."

I got out and watched her drive away. It seemed she wasn't going to park anywhere nearby.

Students crowded outside and everyone was in groups. In the school office, a woman stared at the scars on my face and asked what my name was. I'd seen the look before. She felt sorry for me, whatever. I didn't want to be there. I thought about ditching school altogether that day. I remember thinking: fuck this woman, I hate her. So many teachers and staff at schools tried to feel sorry for me when they first saw me, like something was wrong with me. Fuck her, I thought. She typed my name in on a computer and we waited for my schedule to print. She handed it to me and told me to have a good day and to let her know if I needed anything.

"Seriously, I'll be happy to help you," she said. "Just come by anytime, okay?"

I turned away and walked out. I went into the bathroom and put on eyeliner. Two other guys were in there. One was looking at himself in the mirror, combing his hair. The other guy was leaning against the wall. I could tell he was staring at me.

"Shit, man, what happened to you?"

I ignored him, kept putting on my eyeliner.

"You get your ass kicked?"

The guy combing his hair turned and looked at me. "Whoa, man."

"Eyeliner?" the first guy said. "Do you suck dick?"

I looked at him in the mirror. They both sort of laughed. I stared him down. I didn't care that he was bigger than me. I was ready to fight them if I had to, but they walked out.

I hawked up something from my throat and spat on the mirror. I took my finger and smeared it around. I thought again about ditching, but went ahead to my first class, science. When I walked in, some of the students already in the room stared at me. I saw a couple of girls whispering. I walked past them and sat in the back. The teacher was a wrestling coach. He was a dumpy-looking man, balding, wearing wrinkled brown slacks. "Your brain is like a muscle," he told the class. "The more you put into it, the more it expands."

I went from class to class. Every school I'd been to was the same: people standing in hallways, huddling in groups. I watched everyone drift past, talking in pairs, in deep conversation. Someone ran down the hallway, laughing like a lunatic. Someone else threw a doughnut at the lockers. Nobody paid attention. In my classes I slouched in desks, stared at teachers.

I lost my schedule and had to go back to the office to have it reprinted. While I waited I overheard two teachers talking:

"Listen to all the noise here, the yelling, lockers slamming, loud bells, odd echoes in the halls. The kids are feckless. I need a quiet place, somewhere absent of noise and people. I need a quiet room, a work space without sound. I need to sit in quiet and not think about anything."

The second teacher said, "Did you say feckless?"

"Yes."

"A good solid word."

"Thanks. Are you up for a game of Scrabble? We have twenty minutes left."

At lunch I sat as far away from people as I could. A few other students were at the table with me. I recognized a short kid with green hair from one of my classes. "Welcome to hell," he said. "Does your first day suck?"

"Pretty much," I said.

"It gets worse," he said. His expression never changed.

The kid next to him was poking his milk carton with a straw.

"Do you smoke?" he asked me.

"Sometimes."

"Bring your smokes to school," he said.

They watched me eat. They stared at me the whole time, consumed by my scars, unsure whether I was dangerous or nice. I kept my head down and ate.

"I was totally a fucked-up kid," a girl sitting near us said.

She leaned in and cupped her chin in her hands. "You want to know what happened? I drank drain cleaner a few years ago. It's old news, you know, that was a long time ago. I lost my voice for six months. I'm better now."

Her hands were pale and dry, her nails unpainted and cut short. She talked without hesitation, and I didn't know how to respond. Some boys down the table were laughing, and the noise of the cafeteria made it hard for me to think.

"I was in the hospital for a while after that," she went on. "I couldn't eat anything hard. Lots of soup, ice cream, Jell-O. I didn't mind it at all. All these nurses would come in and immediately they'd feel sorry for me. That's what happens when they find out what you did. They end up doing all sorts of shit for you. What about you? Ever been in the hospital?"

"No."

"I used to be happy," the boy with green hair said.

"Nobody's happy around here," the girl told him. "Everyone would rather be dead."

After lunch I saw two boys fighting by the stairs. A teacher ran down the hall to break it up. Two girls were laughing at me as they walked by.

I overheard some guy say, "Dude, did you see that kid's face?"

I overhead another guy say, "Looks like he was burned."

Another guy said, "Faggot," as he walked past me. I turned and pushed him hard from behind and he fell against a locker. I hit him in the back with my bare hand. He dropped his books and went into a fetal crouch. I wanted to grab him by the hair and pound his face against the locker. Suddenly a crowd of people was around us, watching me. The kid remained crouched down. I couldn't see his face but it appeared he was trying to catch his breath. I was ready for him to come swinging at me. I moved in but the bell rang loudly and everyone rushed past us, hurrying to class. I had a sense of satisfaction. I had never felt this way in such a situation. I turned and went down the stairs to my next class.

As I walked into the classroom, the algebra teacher, whose name was Mr. Gillis, looked at me through thick glasses and asked me my name. His eyes were large and magnified by his lenses. When I told him, he started shuffling through papers on his desk. "Did they send you here?"

I handed him my schedule and he looked at it. "Sequoyah. Sequoyah?"

"Yeah."

"Do you have a book?" he asked.

"What book?"

"The algebra textbook?"

"No."

He stared at me, as if trying to register my response. He looked to the hall, then at my schedule again. He seemed confused. "Sequoyah," he said. "There's an extra textbook here somewhere. What day is this? Go ahead and have a seat."

"Is it a tardy," I asked.

"Is what a tardy?"

"Me."

"Oh," he said. "Oh, it's your first day. You're a new student."

"So no tardy."

"Correct."

I sat in the desk by the window and watched him. He removed his glasses then put them back on. He spent a good minute trying to get everyone's attention, then he turned on the overhead projector and walked over to turn off the lights. The room dimmed and a calmness fell over everyone. A couple of boys in the rows in front of me turned around and looked at my face.

Mr. Gillis sat at the overhead and started writing problems that appeared on the screen. He wrote in green marker despite the fact that one of the students, a girl in black lipstick, reminded him she was color-blind. He stared into the projector. The light illuminated his face. A few students came in late, but he seemed neither aware nor interested. Three or four students in the back of the class were facedown on their desks. A boy was mouthing something to a girl, making smoking gestures.

"Negative six," Mr. Gillis said.

I started feeling sleepy. A boy in the row over from me was sketching a fighter jet on a piece of notebook paper. His concentration was intense. I rested my head on my desk and drowsily watched him. He shaded in details with his pencil. He puckered his face as he drew, really into it. Mr. Gillis squeezed an inhaler into one nostril, which made a horrible sound. I looked away and stared out the window, where a bird was perched on the ledge, preening itself. In the distant sky I saw the dot of a plane drifting slowly into a cloud. The bird suddenly flew away.

Mr. Gillis stared into the blue light of the projector.

"Negative," he kept saying.

Later, during the last period of the day, I saw Mr. Gillis again in the restroom on the third floor. He was standing under the window. I went to the sink and looked at myself in the mirror. I turned on the cold water and washed my hands, drying them afterward with a brown paper towel from the dispenser.

"Hello, Sequoyah," he said. He was looking at me as if waiting for me to say something, but I had nothing to say.

"Don't mind me," he said loudly. "I'm just taking a break, trying to find a quiet place to gather myself after a long day. The teachers' lounge is full of smoke. I'm a conversationalist but not a smoker. What can I say? I'm on meds for severe anxiety. It causes insomnia and stimulates a ringing in my left ear."

He took out his inhaler and sprayed it into both nostrils.

"Nobody wants to talk anymore," he said. "My ex-wife and I used to stay up late in the night talking about everything. Constellations, Sequoyah. Cepheus and Lyra and Aquila in the sky. She made us hot tea and then we played checkers. We played Monopoly, The Game of Life. We talked about adopting kids from Vietnam. Troubled kids. Tell me, what happened to your face?"

I went to the urinal. On the wall in front of me someone had drawn a stick figure holding a gun.

AT THE END OF the school day, George and I had to ride the bus home since Rosemary worked part-time at a thrift store after school. The bus let us out at the edge of Old Fort Road, so we had to walk for a while before we made it home. George lagged behind, out of breath.

"What happens when it rains or snows?" I asked him.

"Pray we don't freeze to death."

Agnes was the only one home when we got there. She was sitting in the living room, crocheting an afghan. "Harold's still at work," she said without looking up. George tossed his backpack on the couch and headed for the kitchen. Agnes looked up at me.

"Are you feeling okay?" she asked. "How was the first day?"

"Everything was fine."

"Are you cold? Can I make you some soup?"

"I'm fine," I said. "I'll go upstairs a while."

"Oh, good idea," she said. "Go upstairs for a while and unwind. Take time for yourself. We'll have dinner around five-thirty."

I went upstairs to the bathroom and sat on the rim of the tub. I took out a cigarette from the pack of Camels I'd kept in my coat for a while. The guy who worked at the mini-mart near the shelter sold them to me.

In the bathroom I lit a cigarette with a lighter and opened the window. I blew smoke out the window and ashed in the toilet. A moment later the door suddenly opened and my heart jumped. I saw Rosemary standing there.

"I didn't know you were in here," she said. "Do you have on eyeliner?"

"Sorry," I said. I dropped the cigarette in the toilet and flushed it. She came in and closed the door behind her, locking it.

"It's cool," she said. "Don't worry, I won't say anything. You have one of those for me?"

I handed her one and lit it for her, then another for myself. I'd seen my mom's boyfriends do it a bunch of times. Women seemed to like it.

"So you smoke too," I said.

"What do you think I do in my room all the time?"

"I guess Harold and Agnes don't know."

"They smoke so they never smell it. They don't know anything. I like the eyeliner."

"I don't think Agnes noticed."

"She's half blind. Both of them are. That's why they don't watch much TV. We don't even have cable TV. They pretend to be religious."

She stopped herself. We both smoked. Her hair hung down and covered part of her face. I sat on the rim of the tub and held my cigarette between two fingers. She sat on the floor with her back to the wall. The silence between us never felt awkward or out of place. The silence was there more to help. Maybe she was thinking about us, that I was someone she could trust. Smoking was our secret from then on. We both knew this and knew we could trust each other.

"What do you mean they pretend?" I asked.

"Harold's a bookie," she said. "Do you know what that is?"

"Yeah."

"People place bets with him almost every day. You'll see him meet with people outside. He leaves at night sometimes. He stays downstairs in the basement and follows the bet line in the newspapers. You'll see all the sports papers if you go down there. It's wild. He doesn't know I know."

"Does Agnes know?"

"How could she not? That must bring in easy money, people paying you all the time."

"But what if they win? Doesn't he pay them?"

"Most people lose," she said. "That's why there's a betting line, to protect the bookie. It gives him the edge. Anyway. Do you read?"

"Yeah, I love to read."

"I have some books in my room. What tribe are you?"

"Cherokee, but only half. My mom calls me Yellow Sky."

"Yellow Sky," she said.

"What tribe are you?"

"Kiowa."

"I know lots of Kiowas from my old school."

"The spirits told me you were coming," she said. "Come to my room later tonight. We'll smoke and I'll show you my books. You should wash your face."

I turned on the faucet in the sink and washed the eyeliner from my face. Rosemary handed me a towel. I dried my face and looked at myself in the mirror. My skin was pale and ghostly. I had darkness under my eyes.

"Tell me how you knew I was coming," I said.

Rosemary took the towel and tossed it onto the floor beside the tub. "A man told me in a dream," she said. "Pay attention to dreams, Yellow Sky."

After dinner that night I went downstairs to the basement where Harold was sitting at his desk, writing on a pad of paper. He looked up when I entered.

"Hello," I said.

He leaned in and inspected his work. "Give me a minute," he said. He consulted a newspaper and wrote something else down. I sat in the chair in front of him and waited for him to finish. He set his pen down and took a drink from his glass. Almost every night he drank a Bloody Mary on the rocks, and there was never a day you wouldn't see a glass on a coffee table or on the counter that had leftover tomato juice and bits of celery in it.

"You follow football, Sequoyah?" he asked.

"Not really."

"Baseball?"

"No."

"Basketball, hockey, tennis? Anything?"

"No."

"I see," he said. "George doesn't either. George doesn't want to watch the Super Bowl. He doesn't care. It's understandable, though. People have different interests." He had a ballpoint pen in his hand that he kept clicking with his thumb. He seemed to be thinking about something.

There was an RCA TV on the table beside him. The basement was full of film reels and VHS tapes on a bookshelf along one wall. Cans of old paint, various tubes, and tools. There were a couple of leather chairs and an older couch against the far wall. When Harold saw me looking at the bookshelf he told me the reels and tapes were mostly football games, the Cowboys and the Steelers. Super Bowls. College bowl games. Also the home movies he'd made since the seventies.

"Agnes and I were young," he said. "I filmed us doing everything. I started with an old 35mm camera, then upgraded to a Zenith a few years ago. I still use it on occasion. They're home movies."

"Home movies," I said.

"I converted most of them to video cassette and keep them down here. We don't watch them anymore but maybe someday."

We heard the phone ring upstairs and Harold looked up toward the door.

I drummed my fingers on the arm of the chair. I felt the

need to talk. There was something comforting about Harold I couldn't figure out. Maybe it was his solitude, or that he talked gently with everyone. He was unlike any man I'd known outside of a male teacher in elementary school, Mr. Lewis, whom I didn't have as a teacher but who always spoke to me and smiled and seemed genuinely friendly.

"School was okay," I told him.

"Your first day. Glad to hear that."

He leaned back in his chair and looked up at the light. "Sometimes I take naps down here," he said. "It's relaxing. I can relax on the couch down here where it's good and quiet. No thumping from Rosie's music upstairs. No typewriter pecking from George working on his book. I'm the only one to take naps anymore. I tell the kids, one day they'll love it. What about you, did you hate naps when you were little?"

"Probably."

"Solitude is good," he said. "Naps, being alone in a room. To be separate from other people and be alone with your thoughts is never a bad thing." He seemed to wait for me to say something, but I had nothing to say.

"For me it's in here," he continued. "I come here every night after dinner. Sometimes in the mornings too. I try to rid myself of all the bad stuff and not worry. It's hard. The best thing I can tell you is to let go of your ego and be kind and giving. George is brilliant. Such a spiritual boy. Last year he read Saint Dimitri's book, and the Upanishads, and some Vedic books. He likes science fiction, too."

I watched him lean forward in his chair. He scratched at his chin, looked at me. He seemed to be looking into me, as if he knew I wanted to listen to him talk about anything.

"It's quiet out here where we live," he said. "We like it this way. Out here in the country you might see possums or skunks. Those kinds of critters."

He sat forward and looked at me. "Little Crow is a good town, Sequoyah. You might see a few strangers, though, like Willie Ray Jones. He walks around with a knapsack full of dirty magazines that he tries to give away to people. If he approaches you, run. Get the hell away from him. About once a week the sheriff or on-duty police officer has to drive him home. Poor guy is cockeyed. He wears a tattered old fedora hat and overalls and work boots even though he doesn't work. He has mental issues and lives with his mother and aunt in a small house behind C.J.'s Seed and Feed. Stay away from him. His mother and aunt drag him along with them to play bingo at the community center every Saturday night. He apparently has to be supervised at all times. His mother, poor woman, has a terrible gambling problem. That's the way it is. She plays bingo and backroom slots at the VFW while Willie takes off all his clothes and walks around town naked. A couple of weeks ago I saw him walking south on Main in only his boxer shorts and boots."

We heard the phone ringing again upstairs. Harold stopped talking and looked up toward the door. I wondered why he was so talkative. Maybe he was trying to develop trust. That was fine with me. For someone who took bets illegally, Harold seemed like a trustworthy guy.

LATE IN THE NIGHT when the house was silent and dark, I tapped on Rosemary's bedroom door. She opened it and put a finger to her lips. I stepped in and she closed it quietly, locking it. Somehow the whole thing felt very mischievous and sexy, but I wasn't sure what her intentions were.

"I owe you a cigarette," she said.

We sat by the open window and smoked. Her room was dim, lit only by a lamp next to her bed. Her wall was decorated with drawings of nude figures and a few posters of rock stars, The Cure, Lou Reed in black lipstick and spiked collar from *Rock N Roll Animal*. A bookshelf on one wall was filled with books.

"I like Human League," I said. "I like Psychedelic Furs."

"Human League is old news, but the Furs are good."

"Did you draw those?" I asked, pointing to the drawings on the wall.

"Yeah. Do you like them?"

"They're good."

"I like nudes. I got an art scholarship to a school on the East Coast for next fall."

"Agnes said something about your interest in painting."

She drew on her cigarette and rested her head back against the wall. I sensed something was wrong but couldn't bring myself to ask. I'd only just met her. I looked out the window and saw the house next door with its dark windows. I saw the empty and dark road beyond. The dead trees, frost on the ground.

We heard a dog howling outside. She told me it was a stray that came around only at night.

"That thing drives me crazy," she said. "Stupid fucking dog."

The dog was barking and howling.

"You were asking about books," she said.

"Yeah."

"I have a couple for you."

She mashed her cigarette in the ashtray and stood. She played a cassette on a stereo beside the bookshelf. I expected music, but instead the tape played a thunderstorm. An ambient noise filled the room, an unidentifiable mixture of wind and rain, followed by the sounds of people crying. Maybe one of the voices was Rosemary on the tape, a recording of her own grief. I imagined her with a group of people, all of them weeping. There's a strange terror in hearing someone grieving. I was too afraid to look at her or see if she was watching me. I stared at the floor while the tape played. When I looked up she was at the bookshelf, picking out a couple of books.

"Is that you?" I asked. "On the tape?"

"It's my friends Sarah and Valerie. They made this one for me. We make tapes for each other."

"But not music."

"Depends. Sometimes we trade music. Sometimes we trade sounds. Whatever we're feeling. I like repetitive sounds. Whispers, rain. This one's sad, but it somehow always makes me feel almost sedated or something."

"It's sad."

"But not really."

She showed me her drawings. The figures contained a sort of distended sleekness: paintings of a crippled man walking with crutches; a hawk with a snake dangling from its beak; a woman wearing a man's tuxedo; a young girl sitting in a chair with her head down as if being punished. Rosemary told me when she was a child she slept on a bed of balsam branches with her brothers and sisters in a small room near Rainy Mountain. She spoke of eating the fried testicles of pigs and cattle and making hides from boarskin, pigskin, and deerskin. Then she handed me two books by N. Scott Momaday, *House Made of Dawn* and *The Way to Rainy Mountain*.

"These," she said. "They're the ones for you. He's from Oklahoma. They're written just for you. If you hate them, everything I've felt about you is wrong and I'll have to go back and reconsider my witchery."

I flipped through one, but it was too dim in the room to read. Both books were paperbacks. I held them in my lap and looked up at her. "Thanks," I said. "You like to read a lot?"

"Drawing and painting are my passions," she said. "Before that I took photos. For days I went around photographing everything: trees, frogs, landscapes, fields. When those photos were developed, the more I looked at them, the more I thought they were really just boring photos and nothing more. There wasn't anything interesting about them. But drawing is different. So tell me your story."

"My story."

"You don't have to tell me anything. I don't know why I asked. I feel a weird connection to you. Do you feel it?"

"I don't know what you mean," I said.

"I felt it when I drove to school. Then again when we were smoking in the bathroom. I can't explain it. Don't think it's like that. I mean it's not like that kind of connection. I mean like you're a lost soul from a thousand years ago who's here to deliver something to me."

"My mom says I'm a reincarnated traveler or something. When I was little I ran away from her all the time. She had to watch me."

"Maybe a Russian pilgrim or monk. It's something like that. Maybe you've felt a strong urgency to find out who I am. Am I right? What I'm interested in, what I want to do with my life, that kind of thing. You want to transcend."

"Hm."

"Am I right?"

"Tell me about your dream," I said. "The one with the man who told you I was coming."

"The dream," she said. "There was a dead man covered in dirt and twigs. He was really dirty. At first I thought he was a windigo or bad spirit. But as he came closer I felt a sense of ease. He said, 'A boy is coming who will help you.' And then he turned and walked away."

"What did he look like?"

"I don't remember. He was covered in so much dirt from the grave. But his voice was soft."

She was staring at me, and I looked away. I knew she was looking at my face, and sure enough, she brought it up. It almost felt inevitable that it would come up. "What happened?" she asked.

"It was an accident," I said. "Hot grease."

She looked sad and leaned in close. I told her the story, emphasizing that it was an accident, and she touched my arm. In that moment I wanted to be close to her, saintly, versed in books. I wanted to immerse myself and be preoccupied with nothing. If I could have any other face, it would be hers. It was very strange like that in the beginning. We shared no physical attraction but something else, something deeper. I saw myself in her. Soon I fell asleep for a while and when I woke she was asleep in her bed. I got up and let myself out, closing her door quietly. When I got to my room, George was asleep in his bed. He turned his back to me as I entered.

There was a note on my bed in George's handwriting: *Goodnight to my new friend.* I settled back on my bed and stared up at the pale light and thought about dying. George was making explosion noises with his mouth. The room was colorless and spectral, a space where nothing happened. If I died in bed, I would lie there with cold skin until someone found me. I thought the room was dreaming and I was the subject of the room's dream. I thought of myself being devoured by my bed. I was the bed's baby. I was the offspring, about to be eaten, killed by the bed.

I drifted in and out of sleep. At some point in the night I looked at the doorway and saw a figure in the shape of my mother.

I never had many friends. In Cherokee County, I knew a boy named Monfiori who lived in the neighborhood. He was pale-skinned and thin with wiry hair. Everyone at school hated him, but for a while he was my only companion. He ate cock-roaches for a dollar and huffed paint behind the woodshop building. He smoked cigarettes in my bedroom despite my weak lungs and my coughing. My mother was worried people would think I was a troublemaker for being friends with him.

"We're like hemophiliac brothers," Monfiori said. "They tell us don't bleed, don't bleed, but we're dying anyway. They don't know anything."

"I'm not a hemophiliac," I told him.

Somehow he didn't believe me. He'd made comments about the burn marks on my face, that I needed to watch out in case they ever bled me to death.

"That'll never happen," I told him. "They're scars."

He refused to believe me. He played jazz on a toy trumpet. "Variations on Monk in C," his own creation, this arrangement—or so he claimed. "Psychedelic funk," he called it. We drank cheap vodka in his basement, and I played drums on upside down buckets. I liked being at his house because I could drink and smoke over there without anyone knowing.

"My mom has jazz records," I told him. "She listens to them on nights she wants to be left alone."

"She'll be alone soon enough when you die," he said.

Monfiori said we were both dying. "Might as well poison ourselves," he said. "At least that way we'll die in our sleep." He'd already gotten two blood transfusions. He had bruises and moles all over his body. I saw the moles on his cheek and neck. His hair hung in his eyes and always looked unkempt, but I liked it. He was probably the ugliest boy in our school, and maybe the meanest.

One time in his basement we smoked a joint and he told me he was going to set the school on fire. "We'll watch the whole place go up in flames," he said. "I'll send smoke signals to the Indians. Fuck the police and everyone else."

Monfiori and I had to do twenty hours of community service for stealing guitar strings from the music store downtown. We were going to use them to tie the spokes and chain of his brother's bicycle so that he would crash. Monfiori's mom and aunt caught us later in his backyard as we were tying the strings to the spokes. They made us return the packages of guitar strings to the music store. The owner wanted to press charges and we had to go to juvenile court.

"My son's not a bad kid," my mother kept telling everyone.

That same winter I fell ill with a stomach virus and my asthma flared up. The breathing machine they had me use was loud enough to hear throughout the house. At night the dogs next door kept me awake with their barking. They belonged to our neighbors, who were an old couple, immigrants from Poland. Their names were Milosz and Gertrude. They brought me soup and crackers and a dessert called *faworki*, which they said was known as angel wings.

"They're for good luck," Gertrude told me. "It's a Polish specialty."

My mother and Gertrude became close. They talked about bread and sausages and red wine. Milosz made paper airplanes for me. From my bed, in my sickness, I watched him pull up a chair. He folded a piece of paper into an airplane and tossed it across the room.

"I had a son once," Milosz told me. "My wife and I lost him. He was about your age."

He stared into the floor. He seemed to be searching for the right words. We could hear my mother and Gertrude laughing in the next room.

"His name was Aleksander," he said. "He liked to play the piano."

I could see the lines in his forehead, the loose skin of his jowls.

"My son, my son," he said.

He folded another piece of paper. I watched his fingers

move, all bone and skin. He concentrated on each fold, creasing it, holding it up to the light to make sure he got it right. He folded the paper into a bird and handed it to me.

"You can name it anything you want," he said.

"Aleksander," I said.

I held the paper bird. I noticed Milosz's hands were trembling.

"Aleksander it is," he said. He stared into the floor.

Those days I was sick I would often see a male cardinal appear on the branch outside my window. One morning I opened the window and he flew in. He was such a beautiful bird. He flew wildly around my room. He glided from desk to bedpost, from bookshelf to lampshade. His wings were red like velvet. He was proud but silent. He seemed to be attentive to some inner presence, as if he had a clear point to make as he strutted across the windowsill. Once, he spread his wings proudly for me. This was his own show, a brief abandonment of the natural world, his own strange fantasy. The last time I saw him, that winter day I was ill, he flew in and shook the frost from his body. I let him eat sugar from my hand. In the pale light of my bedroom, in one final, cool gesture of farewell, he cocked his head to look at me, then flew out the window.

For several weeks Milosz continued to bring me paper birds made from colored construction paper. I hung them with string from my ceiling so that they twirled constantly. There were red birds, blue birds, yellow birds, purple birds. Monfiori didn't like them. "Can we set them on fire?" he asked.

"No."

"Aren't you too old for this? Look at this place."

He challenged my integrity. He dared me to cut myself and bleed. I challenged him back and he laughed it off. One Friday I stayed the night at his house. We drank his mother's vodka until late. I fell asleep on the floor in his basement and woke up at some point in the middle of the night, feeling sick. I found him sitting in the corner of the room, watching me.

"What is it?" I asked.

He mumbled something.

"What's wrong with you?" I said.

"We're both dying," he said. "We'll die together."

I was sick the whole next day. In my room, Milosz sipped wine and told me stories about a boy who kept birds to fend off devils. "The birds protected him," he said. "They changed colors and held healing powers, like tiny gods or angels. They showed courage. They taught the boy to believe in himself."

Milosz wheezed and coughed. I coughed, too. His glass of red wine seemed to glow in the dim room. The paper birds twirled above our heads.

One night I woke to something knocking at my window. I sat up in bed, pulled back the curtain but saw nothing. Outside, the wind was blowing. It was a tree branch, I told myself, and went back to sleep.

Later I dreamed of the cardinal at my window. The cardinal spread his wings, glowing red in the night.

Weeks passed and Monfiori left my life as quickly as he'd

entered. I saw him for the last time later that winter. We sat in his basement drinking cheap vodka and smoking cigarettes. I watched him wrestle his little brother to the floor and punch him in the chest until the boy started crying and ran out of the room.

"You need to stop being mean," I told him.

"I'm not," he said. "We're dying, so what does it matter?"

He turned on the strobe light. We stayed up late in the night listening to some sort of death metal, all screams and guitar. I remember slamming my body into the wall. I remember lying on the floor and pulling a blanket over myself.

I'm convinced he tried to poison me in my sleep. The next morning they found me unresponsive. I don't remember being carried out of the house, the ambulance ride, or anything else. I woke up in a hospital bed on the third floor of Southwest Central Hospital, where they watched me for several days. There, my mother kept telling the nurses I wasn't a bad kid. They fed me tapioca pudding. They helped me out of bed and tried to talk to me, but I wanted to be left alone. I watched cartoons and old movies on TV.

"He's a quiet kid," one of the nurses told my mother. "He never talks."

When I returned home, the first people who came to see me were Milosz and Gertrude. They brought me angel wings. We drank tea and listened to old records on the antique record player. I mostly kept to myself in my bedroom.

My mother said Monfiori had tried to hang himself and they took him away. He wouldn't be coming back for a while.

"That boy is nothing like my son," my mother told Milosz and Gertrude. "He was trouble, it's so sad," she said.

They all agreed I was nothing like him.

"My son is very happy," my mother kept saying.

AT THE TROUTTS, WE usually ate dinner around six in the evening. Rosemary ate alone in her room and nobody questioned it. I saw it as some sort of healing mechanism for her that required no explanation. Maybe the conversation had been exhausted. Maybe they gave up. Every night around ten, Harold came upstairs from the basement and watched the evening news before he went upstairs to bed. Agnes always sat in the same recliner in the living room, reading the Bible or some book on spirituality.

Since the night Rosemary had given me the books, I became more and more drawn to her. As the only Indians around, we shared a culture and blood unknown to the others. We were like branches intertwined from the same tree, the same root, reaching out toward the sky to the unknown. I felt drawn to her as a brother is to a lost sister, nothing more. Maybe I felt too strongly. I see now that I tended to get attached easily, but at the time I felt it was necessary to be near her, watch her, even protect her if I needed to. I kept all this to myself.

George, however, became unbearable with all his eccentricities. He paced, muttered to himself, continually asked me questions about where I came from. Nights he continued to make explosion noises with his mouth, keeping me awake. He stayed in his room, writing notes in a notebook and memorizing the birthdates of rock stars. One afternoon after school he wanted me to tell him about the Cherokees, so I told him about the Trail of Tears, which he was learning about in his Oklahoma History class. I spoke the words of a song one of my mother's boyfriends had taught me, written many years ago by some unknown Cherokee man:

I am a proud Cherokee, don't take away my land.
Don't take away my land, this here is Cherokee land.
I'm a proud Cherokee, don't take away my land,
You mean old white man.

I got a bottle full of wine, some rum and whiskey too.
I'm a-gonna get drunk on rum and whiskey, too.
I'm a-gonna get drunk, and I'll show you what I'll do,
You mean old white man.

When your train comes to town, you better go away.
You better go away, you took my land away.
I'm a-gonna get drunk, you better go away,
You mean old white man.

George wrote the lyrics in his notebook. When he was finished he asked what key it was in. "It's like a folk song?" he asked. "Is it played on acoustic guitar?"

"I think so. I don't know."

"Sounds like a folk song," he said.

He set the notebook down and looked up to the ceiling, then back to the floor. "Rosemary's in the woods with some guy," he said.

I sat up in bed. "In the woods?"

"She goes there to draw. She draws in the woods."

"But with a guy?"

"She draws naked people," he said. "I've seen her drawings. She draws naked men and women. Do you want to see them? I know where they are in her room."

"Why do they go to the woods?" I asked.

He pulled on his lower lip, staring at the floor.

"George," I said.

"To draw, to draw," he said.

I went downstairs and put on my coat. As I walked by the kitchen window I saw Rosemary and a boy standing outside in the backyard. She was holding her large sketchbook and they were talking. I stood there watching them for a moment. Rosemary was saying something. The boy laughed and then Rosemary laughed. Then they started to walk toward the woods.

I slipped out the back door and followed them. I stayed back and entered the woods far behind them, taking the winding path around a stand of trees to an area where I could stay secluded and watch. They didn't know I was there. I crouched next to a bush, among a scattering of leaves and twigs, and watched Rosemary sit cross-legged on the ground with her sketchbook in her lap while the boy sat across from her, resting against a tree. I saw the boy slumped forward, grinding his boots into the dirt while he waited for her to take out her pencils and get comfortable. I saw Rosemary's dark hair spilling down her back. I saw the way she was sitting there staring at him before she ever started drawing. Watching her, I was struck with a feeling of betrayal, or maybe abandonment for whatever reason, and I found myself feeling overly anxious and confused.

Then she started drawing him, and I leaned forward to rest my elbows on a stump and watched. I was very still and quiet. The boy said something to Rosemary, but I couldn't hear what he said. They talked for a moment, and I heard her say, "Be still, you idiot!" Then they fell quiet again as she stared at him and began drawing. He had not taken off his clothes, but I imagined he had. And I imagined Rosemary had, too, so that they were both naked and alone, unaware of any other presence. In that space of time, while she drew, I entered both Rosemary and the boy and allowed them to move the way I wanted them to. I moved his body to meet hers. His body was spindly and pale. Rosemary's skin was dark against his. He crouched down to kiss her navel and she laughed. And I, too, laughed as they collapsed to the ground in the gray light suffusing through the cold afternoon. The bitter cold never bothered them, not in their sudden passion.

And I heard their unmistakably human cries, full of pleasure, thin in the dusty sky. I heard Rosemary's voice, full of wonder, strange and mysterious, cries that rang out against the branches. And I thought about this for what seemed like a long while, sitting there resting my elbows on the stump, and everything around me felt incongruous and warm. I turned away yet still desired her. The air filled with the sweetness of fruit, and I could not contain myself from the dizzy exhaustion of the moment.

I slipped quietly away. I walked back to the house and found Agnes inside, smoking by the window. The ashtray was filled with cigarette butts. She snubbed out her cigarette and tried to smile.

"What's she doing out there?" she asked me.

"Who?"

"Rosemary. Didn't you see her?"

"Oh," I said. "Oh. I saw her with her sketchbook, drawing some guy. That was all."

"They're still there? Why did you leave?"

"Bored, I guess."

Agnes sighed with pain, as if she were feeling ill. She looked worried. I had no idea why, and I didn't ask.

I went upstairs to the bedroom and started reading one of the books Rosemary had given me. Momaday's bio on the back cover said he was from right here in Oklahoma. I really liked the book and that he was an Indian like us.

George was sitting at his desk, drawing something using colored markers. He sometimes designed his own greeting cards and handed them out at school. He'd memorized a number of his classmates' birthdays, as well as several teachers', so he always made sure to give them a part of himself. The drawings were usually abstract symbols with letters or numbers signifying something about their relationship. I found it fascinating, really. Whenever he worked on a project like this he remained quiet and focused, which I liked because I was able to read in peace.

Soon I heard a car start outside. I looked out the window and saw Rosemary sitting in the passenger's seat of the boy's car. The car pulled out of the drive and drove away. I set the book on the windowsill, put my coat on and went downstairs. Agnes wasn't in the living room or kitchen when I walked by, but I could smell the cigarette smoke in the air. I went outside and walked all the way back to the woods, to the spot where Rosemary had been drawing the boy. I wasn't sure why I felt the need to be there or what I hoped would happen. It felt colder now. The wind swelled, and I saw snails crawling in the dirt while branches all around me trembled. Among all this, I felt Rosemary's presence.

A radiant blue, chilly afternoon, I stood silently watching her from the kitchen window while she sat on the back patio with her friend, Nora Drake. Nora, who avoided eye-contact with me, always. Nora, who Rosemary later told me assumed I'd developed a crush on Rosemary that was creepy and borderline dangerous. She laughed it off, thankfully. As I stood at the window I saw them both sitting in plastic chairs at the patio table, both drinking from cans of soda and talking about something that was making Nora burst into laughter every so often. Rosemary was wearing sunglasses and a black sweater with blue jeans and black shoes. An old pair of tennis shoes rested on the patio by her feet, and on the table there was an opened photo album they were both flipping through, looking at photos. For a while I watched, oblivious to whether anyone could've been in the room or standing near me. Rosemary had both hands placed on the album and was leaning in close to Nora, saying something that seemed of great importance, when the phone rang. It was Liz, calling to ask how things were going.

"The school said you're doing well," she said. "I'm glad to hear that. Are you doing okay?"

"I like it here," I said. "They're nice people."

"And the two others? Are you getting along with them?"

"I like them."

"That's good," she said. "I wanted to remind you that your mother's hearing is next month. I'm going to request supervised visits if she's released."

I didn't say anything. It all felt too heavy over the phone, thinking about my mother being released and returning home.

"You think she'll be released?" I asked.

"I'm not sure. There's always a chance she will be."

After we hung up, I watched Rosemary and Nora walk to Nora's car and drive away.

While they were gone, I went upstairs and snuck into Harold and Agnes's bedroom. I looked around on the dresser for something to pick Rosemary's lock with, but I couldn't find anything. I stepped into their bathroom and looked through Agnes's makeup, where I found a hairpin. I carefully went out and down the hall to Rosemary's door, where I eventually picked the lock. It was something I'd done at our house in Cherokee County whenever my mother was working and I wanted to snoop through her room for cigarettes. I didn't sneak in to steal anything. I wanted to look around for something, but I had no idea what it was.

Thinking back on it, this was the first time I'd seen her

bedroom alone. Her room was a place of mysterious elements, and I felt wildly alive as I searched through it, from
wall to wall, shelf to shelf, corner to corner. There, objects
became whole, and I slowly felt deep within myself a desire
I couldn't understand. It was confusing, really, I wasn't sure
what I was feeling.

Her room, unorganized and cluttered, in no specific order.
There were cassette tapes and teen magazines. Her music
collection was eclectic if not popular for the time: Duran
Duran, Depeche Mode, Joni Mitchell, Johnny Cash—along
with various mixes she had titled such as "Mix for Jessie" and
"Mix for Holly" and "Mix for DMH." Her books were shelved
in no discernable order. Dirty clothes were scattered on the
floor. Like a lunatic I got down on my hands and knees and
searched under her bed, where I found two bins. I slid them
out and went through both, which were full of random items,
including old bracelets and rings and necklaces, some photos
of her as a child with a thin woman in bell-bottom pants and
long, dark hair—her mother, I assumed—along with a nail file,
nail polish, beads, hair clips, buttons, one golden earring, an
old spiral notebook with blank pages, and a cigarette lighter.

There were also colored pencils, markers, colored chalk,
and watercolor paint. There were scraps of paper full of
doodles and scribbles—on one page her signature was written
repeatedly in various colors; on another, the name "Nora"
was written several times, in cursive, more carefully than her
own name. I found one pink mitten. I found a greeting card

with a picture of two kittens pawing playfully at each other; inside the card, which read "You Are Purrrfect!" someone had added, "I miss you," in ballpoint pen, the handwriting surely female—but there was no signature. The card smelled of raspberry, maybe, or lemon. There were also some blue and red ribbons, first and second place in an art show. I found a T-ball medal and a soccer ball keychain. All this, under the bed.

In one of the notebooks I discovered a medical form of some sort:

NORTHRIDGE NEUROLOGICAL INSTITUTE
COMPREHENSIVE PROGRAM FOR EPILEPSY
AUDIO-VISUALLY MONITORED EEG REPORT
Blackwell, Rosemary
E0293794573
INTERPRETATION:

The recording showed two events during monitoring. Both events indicated that the patient experienced no epileptic episodes or numbness of sensations in the head and body. There were also no delayed responses. The patient was able to mumble excessively at various points of time and also respond to the EEG technologist.

Two events were reported:

Event #1 was logged at 0932 and indicated that the patient was lying in a supine position without any facial activity or noticeable movements of the upper or lower extremities. The EEG technologist logged a response at

0938 as the patient responded by mumbling something unintelligible. The patient was also able to open her mouth in response to the EEG technologist, as well as nod her head. There was no verbal response except for the excessive mumblings. At 0941, the EEG technologist logged this event as a nonelectrogenic (pseudo) seizure.

Event #2 was logged at 1126. Patient was lying in a supine position and began moving lower extremities in response to the EEG technologist. The patient's only facial activity was a slight opening of the mouth before mumbling. The patient managed to mumble incoherently during this event. The EEG technologist noted extreme facial activity during this mumbling. This event, unlike the first, was not logged as an electrogenic (pseudo) seizure. The EEG showed an awake background pattern during both of these events and indicated that no epileptic episodes had occurred.

I wasn't sure if this meant Rosemary was epileptic or what. I found some writing in the notebook, in purple ink:

Last night I asked too many questions about things like mice. Our house has them and Mom has traps scattered everywhere! Mom sits in the living room studying Zoology or something from the community college. She went into a long explanation about how mice had been used in genetic experiments to aid in scientific studies. She once bought me an encyclopedia set and went through it with me whenever

I asked questions like this, but mostly I just looked at the illustrations and pictures. I like to look at Michelangelo's statue of David. Ancient tombs. All the diagrams of bodies. The human body. <u>*I wonder what my body will look like when I die?*</u>

The last line, underlined. Where was the rest? The other pages from this entry had been torn out, but a few pages later I found this strange list:

What I learned from juvenile detention:
All the guards wore jeans rather than slacks so their keys wouldn't slide out of their pockets whenever they sat down on the couches. "Code ten" means an emergency, and "delivery" means the police had brought a kid in. Staff never wore any necklaces. Maybe they thought someone would try to choke them. A few boys peed on the floor in the bathroom. Guards working the night shift checked on us every 15 fucking minutes. Prostitution is worse than I thought. Most of us participated in weekly Bible studies. I think I was maybe the smartest person there. A boy had to be treated for lice. One night he barked like a dog to get the staff to think he was crazy so he could get out of detention and go to the hospital for a mental evaluation. It sucks. The reason I had to squat and cough during the intake was because some residents try to smuggle in drugs or money in their assholes. That's what a staff member

told me anyway. I never saw a fight. Staff counted all the pencils and silverware. Maybe they thought we would stab someone or screw with the locks. Nobody tried to kill anyone. Nobody tried suicide.

Other pages were ripped out. There was no other writing— only this. What had she done to get locked up? I put the notebook back in the bin and slid it under the bed.

The room was like a treasure-house. I crawled from the bed to the mahogany bookshelf. I crawled from the bookshelf to the closet, where she kept her clothes and shoes. I went through her dresser drawers, through T-shirts, socks, pants, undergarments. I wasn't sure what I was looking for. The room lit up like stained glass. I saw blues, greens, yellows, and reds. I wanted to touch as many things of hers as possible. I touched her comforter, her pillows. I touched her clothes and the wooden handles on her closet doors.

Her closet was filled with clothes on hangers. I ran my hand over her shirts and pants, over her blue jeans and skirts. Shoes were scattered about on the floor. Sweaters were folded on a shelf above. On one of the hangers I found a black button-down cardigan sweater. I took it off the hanger and put it on. The sleeves were a little long, but it fit well, I noticed, as I leaned in close and looked at myself in the mirror above her dresser. I put on my eyeliner, using short, brief strokes beginning at the inside corner of my eye and ending at the outer corner. I drew upwards at the outer corner toward my eyebrow to create a cat eye. I did this with both eyes, then I sat on the bed, hugging myself in her sweater.

I fantasized about Rosemary being naked on the bed. I thought about sticking an object inside her and fucking her with it until it hurt her. I thought of making her bleed. But this never aroused me. I was never sexually attracted to her in this way, yet I liked thinking about her in that sort of pain. I thought of her aching. I thought of watching her fold over the bed, blood running down her legs.

From the bookshelves, the nightstand and dresser, and from the corners of the room, I noticed little figurines and dolls watching me. The dolls were antiques in faded white dresses, with closed mouths and dark eyelashes. Their eyes stared at me. The little figurines—the porcelain matador on the bookshelf, wearing a green hat and holding his red cape, the white rabbit standing on hind legs, and the two matching clowns wearing baggy green and blue pajama-like outfits, their faces painted white and their noses red, both holding a black top hat with rabbit ears protruding out—all were watching me. They had watched me rummaging about the room on my hands and knees. I wanted to break all of them, shatter them to pieces.

When I stood I saw my reflection in the mirror above her dresser. I saw a couple of Polaroids hidden underneath some music magazines. They were photos of Rosemary. One revealed her lying in bed with her face turned into the pillow. You couldn't see her face. She was in only her bra and underwear, her wrists and ankles tied with rope. In the second one she was more in a fetal position, crouched with her wrists tied behind her back. I was neither aroused nor bothered, though I liked that I could see the bones of her spine in one of the photos.

I replaced them underneath the magazines and went over to one of the dolls and touched its hair, which felt coarse and stiff. The doll stared at me with big eyes. With a finger I poked around on its body: the eyelashes, the nose, the mouth, all the delicate parts.

THE DAY LUMBERED ON without her. Harold was gone, Agnes was running errands, and George was particularly quiet, staying to himself downstairs until he finally came up to the room and, without saying anything, began writing in his notebook. I started writing myself—a letter to my mother, but I stopped after a few sentences, writing only: *Dear Mom, guess what? School's going ok.* I started daydreaming about her life in jail and what she did all day, eating and sleeping in her cell. I wrote: *I'm not sure what to think about anything. I'm not even sure who I am. School is weird sometimes. Who are these people? I miss you.*

Then I heard a car door shut outside. I went to the window and peered out. Rosemary got out of Nora's car and walked to the door. My breath left a circle of fog on the window.

"What do you know about Nora?" I asked George.

George stopped writing and looked up at me. "Nothing

really," he said. "She doesn't talk to me. She doesn't look at me. I don't know."

"I get the feeling she doesn't like me," I said.

"She doesn't like me either. She doesn't like anyone except Rosemary."

The light in the room was fading. Outside, the sky was turning gray with rain clouds. My head was hurting, and for a while I lay on my bed with my arm over my face. George started talking about needing twigs for a school project but that he didn't want to go into the woods.

"I need five sticks, all different lengths," he said. "Can you get them for me?"

"I've had a headache that keeps getting worse. Can't you go?"

"I'd rather you go."

"What is it about the woods that bothers you?"

He was writing something in his notebook. I waited for him to answer, but he chose not to.

Finally I went downstairs, expecting to find Rosemary, but she wasn't there. Agnes was talking on the phone in the kitchen to someone in a low voice. Harold hadn't gotten home from work yet. I put on my coat and went outside and walked to the woods alone. I stopped and picked up a rock and tossed it toward a tree. The rock hit a branch and fell. By the time I made it to the woods I happened to notice Rosemary up ahead. She was sitting on a stump, drawing. She looked up and saw me.

"I didn't know you were here," I said.

"It's okay," she said. "I like to come here to draw sometimes. It's the quiet I like, and nature."

"George needs some sticks for a project at school," I said.

I stood close to her in the woods, in the cool, rising wind of an approaching storm. She sat on the stump with her skirt hiked high above her knees, the sketchbook in her lap. I started gathering twigs.

"You should make him do it himself," she said.

"He wanted to be alone."

"George always wants to be alone. He'll go to extreme lengths to be by himself. He once made an entire map of places where he could be by himself."

I knelt down to the ground and looked in the dirt. "He wants five sticks of different lengths. It's hard to find good ones and my head hurts."

"You have a headache?" she asked.

"I've been getting them lately. I don't know. Maybe more water."

"More water," she said. "I used to get them a lot, too. I had an EEG done once to determine if I was having seizures. I saw flashes of light. I blacked out sometimes. It turned out to be anxiety and stress."

She held her exposed knees together and scribbled in her sketchbook. She slouched, her hair tangled and covering part of her face as she drew. With the dim light slanting in on her through the trees, I could almost feel what it was like to be a part of her, inside her, not stifled in my own world, not confused but certain of purpose, sitting there entranced. Maybe in a weird way I wanted to be her.

"I have to pee," she said. She looked up at me.

"I can go back," I said.

She set the sketchbook beside her and stood. "I don't care," she said. "You can watch. Do you want to watch me pee?"

I watched her hike up her skirt and squat in the woods. She turned her head, wiped her mouth with the back of her hand. A cold air hung in the shadows as her hands moved up her thighs. Dead leaves curled around her feet and the edges of the tree beside her, and I envisioned myself embracing her in that moment.

When she finished and stood I noticed how peculiarly innocent she appeared in her skirt, with a slim waist and broad hips. This is mostly how I remember her: pure in Indian blood, lovely, dressed in the late day sky. How well she knew this. And I was a young boy staring at her.

She hugged herself and shivered a moment. "It's getting cold," she said. "My hands are freezing. Come feel my hands."

I walked to her and took her hands in mine. Her fingers were cold and fragile, like a child's hands might feel. Taking her hands in mine made me feel stronger than her.

"You have leaves in your hair," she said, pulling something out of my hair.

"Yeah, but I'm clean."

She leaned in and studied me for a moment.

"You smell like duck feathers," she said.

She laughed and I stepped back and looked down, where I saw a dead bird. Her laughter, I can still hear it. Her laughter came out of nowhere. Angry, I turned and walked back to the house. I kept walking without looking back at her. Dead leaves and twigs cracked under my feet and the wind blew in circular gusts. The sky had gone dead gray. What made me even angrier was that, as I walked away, she wasn't calling after me.

Every night we ate dinner in silence, which seemed to be normal. I was used to eating in front of the TV or with other kids at the shelter laughing and being loud. During dinner, Harold stirred his Bloody Mary with his finger and stared into his glass. Then Agnes said to him, "Jim and Marjorie are having a get-together this weekend."

"The swingers," he said.

"They're not swingers. Are they swingers? I don't think they're swingers."

"I'm positive they're swingers," he said. "Burt was talking about it the other day at the gym."

"Burt. What does Burt know? Marjorie's son is going to France to study abroad."

Harold spoke without looking at anyone. "France? Good for him. He's the one with the seborrheic dermatitis?"

"Who has dermatitis?"

"And they're having a party."

"Jim called me today. We should take a bottle of wine. We need to go."

Harold sipped his Bloody Mary. I saw the bits of pepper in his glass, tiny pieces of celery. "I need to fix that light fixture," he said.

Agnes said, "Harold, I need you to listen to me."

"The swingers, the swingers."

I looked at George, who kept his head down, eating. He didn't seem distracted by the conversation.

"Please," Agnes said.

Harold looked at me, then at George. He looked at his food. He looked up at the light fixture. He looked at everything except Agnes.

"Look," Agnes said.

"It doesn't work," Harold said, sipping his drink. He leaned back in his chair and squinted.

Agnes stood from the table and started taking the dishes into the kitchen. The three of us sat there, not saying anything.

"Can we go upstairs?" George asked, looking at his food.

"Of course," Harold said.

George and I rushed from the table and hurried upstairs.

Later the thunderstorm hit, which made me sad. Thunderstorms still do this to me, years later, they tend to send me into a deep emptiness. As it rained I went to lie down on the bed. For a while I tried to read, but I had a headache. George came over and handed me a note. It said: *You are very quiet.*

"I'm reading," I said. "Why don't you just talk? Rosemary said you made a map of secret places. Can you show it to me?"

"They aren't secret places, they're quiet places. I can show you."

He went to his dresser and got a notebook from the top drawer. He opened it to the page and brought it over to me. "There's a bunch more on another page somewhere, but I lost it. Or maybe Agnes threw it away or someone stole it, I don't know."

The page showed an outline of the basement floor of the school, with an arrow pointing behind a staircase. I turned the page and saw a map of the public library, all three floors, with arrows pointing to tables in the corners of the rooms.

"Technically the library's pretty quiet everywhere, but I have my favorite areas where you can disappear. The missing pages include maps of Birch Park and the underground tunnels near Katachee Hill."

"You like to be alone," I said.

"People are mean," he said.

"I know. They can be terrible."

"What happened to your face?"

The abruptness of the question caught me off guard. I had assumed Harold or Agnes had already spoken to him about it, but evidently they hadn't.

"It was an accident," I said.

"Burned?"

"Yeah, hot grease was spilled. It was an accident."

He was waiting for me to continue, to tell the story, but I didn't want to. "I need some aspirin," I said.

I went downstairs to the kitchen and took two aspirin. In the dining room, Harold and Agnes were now playing cards. Harold asked if I wanted to sit with them, so I did. They didn't invite me to play—only to sit there and watch. Agnes seemed bothered by something. Harold studied his cards while Agnes stared at him.

"I'm waiting," she said. "Harold."

"Yeah," he said.

"I'm waiting for you to make a move, Harold."

"I'm thinking about the swingers," he told her.

Harold took a drink of his Bloody Mary and swished it around in his mouth. Agnes stared at him.

"Let's just quit," she finally said, and stood from the table.

"Take it easy," Harold told her.

"Holy mother!" she yelled. "Go do whatever you want." She walked out of the room.

I couldn't bear to look at Harold, but I knew he was looking at me to see my response.

"It is what it is," he said quietly.

It was the first time I'd seen Agnes angry. George had told me she kept her emotions hidden well, and that Harold and her made sure not to fight much in front of anyone. There were periods of time she spent alone in their bedroom. Other times she went for a drive. "I need alone time," she sometimes said. It wasn't every night, but it was frequent.

At the table, I wasn't sure what to do, so I sat there. I knew this: I liked living there. I knew it was a safe place isolated in the country, near Snake River. I understood when I looked around the room and noticed how everything around me felt important. At the shelter everything had felt cold and dead and lonely. The rooms were hollow and held a sadness I couldn't bear. There was no color anywhere. But the Troutts' house felt alive. I looked at the pictures on the wall, pictures of Harold and Agnes, of a stream in the woods, a watercolor of geese flying low over water, and it felt hypnotic. I liked the open window, where I could see the land stretching outside. I liked the light blue curtains. I liked the arrangement of tulips in thin glass vases.

Harold was handsome the way he held his glass in front of his face and stared at it. He began talking about his father. It was his way of opening up to me, I guess. "My father never spent much time with me," he said. "He worked as an editor for a university textbook publishing company and spent his days sitting alone in a small room in a very old building. Two nights a week he taught a class to undergraduates on methods of research. Dull. His office was dim and colorless and always had a strange odor that was difficult to define."

He looked at me over his glass. "There was a 1950s décor with wood paneling on the walls and thin carpet on the floor," he continued. "His desk was metal and stacked with papers, books and pamphlets and several sharpened pencils. What a dull space. The motorized grind of pencils sharpening in the electric pencil sharpener was the only sound my father ever heard in that office outside the ticking of the clock on the wall. The clock was the large kind typical of most classrooms, the only thing he had on the wall behind his desk. There was one family picture on his desk. Coworkers suggested he buy a radio, but that would've been a distraction. And my father was easily distracted. He was a dull man. He ate his lunch alone at his desk and only twice a day took a break to get up and walk upstairs to the watercooler. There, he occasionally spoke to coworkers, but only if prompted."

I didn't know how to respond, so I just nodded.

"He was never a conversationalist," he said. "He was polite and soft-spoken and took his work seriously. He wore a well-starched shirt with a breast pocket where he kept his favorite ballpoint pen. One day he got let go. They didn't need him anymore. He became severely depressed. Then he opened up a little backdoor gambling place on the outskirts of town with his brother, and after that he was a new man. It was illegal, but the cops didn't mind. Not out there. He took a chance and started doing what he wanted to do. I learned a lot from that."

He had dark eyes and a manner about him that reminded me of a movie star from an old film from the 1950s or '60s, and I found myself staring at him.

A moment later Rosemary came downstairs and sat next to Harold at the table. She glanced at me, but I turned away. I was still angry about her comment in the woods.

"I was looking for you," she told Harold. He looked at his watch, and Rosemary rested her head against his shoulder. It was a very daughterly thing to do, I remember thinking, especially for a foster daughter. A simple gesture of affection. For a minute I sat there, looking at my hands.

"Agnes is in the other room praying," she said.

"It is what it is," Harold said.

It came to me that Rosemary had been listening to us, maybe the whole time, and now I could feel her watching me.

"Is your head feeling better?" she asked.

"What's wrong with your head?" Harold said.

"He had a bad headache earlier," Rosemary said.

I excused myself and went back upstairs. In our room, George was lying on his bed with the light off. I lay in my bed in the dark with my hands behind my head. The wind was blowing the tree outside my window. With the lights off, George and I must've looked gray as ghosts in the moonlit room. I could see the streetlight reflecting through the branches of the elm outside my window. George and I lay silent for a while until he finally sat up in bed and turned on his lamp.

"I've been thinking," he said. "I used to be afraid of the shed out back. It started last winter when we found rats in the shed. Harold put down poison and got rid of them, but I kept imagining a whole community of rats living below ground. Rats crawling around. Rats standing upright on their back legs, smoking pipes and watching the world above them, where we lived. Rats digging tunnels of their own, designing a whole underground transportation system. I thought the shed was their door to the human universe."

"Weird," I said.

"I know. It took going in there a bunch of times, but I'm better now. I started counting the bricks in the floor out there, which helped."

We were quiet. I could hear the wind outside the window.

"I need to show you something tomorrow," he said. "Something in the shed."

"What is it? A rat?"

"No. I'd show you now but it's too dark. Tomorrow. Okay?"

"All right," I said.

A few minutes later Rosemary appeared at the door. She leaned against the doorjamb and crossed her arms. "Sorry about earlier," she said.

She held my gaze, waiting for me to respond, and as she did I got the feeling she was accustomed to making these types of apologies and getting a response. And yet I couldn't say anything, or maybe it wasn't the right moment, so I looked back at my book until she walked away. It was hard to concentrate on reading, though, and for whatever reason I felt guilty for not accepting her apology.

After that I distracted myself with cleaning, spraying, and wiping the windows, dusting the bookshelf and dressers, picking up the clothes from the floor and carrying the hamper into the laundry room down the hall. In the bathroom I brushed my teeth and flossed until my gums bled. I gargled with green Listerine that burned so badly my eyes watered. Then I undressed and took a long shower until the bathroom filled with steam.

George was knocking on the door, asking if everything was okay. I called out that I was taking a shower. He knocked again, asking if I had a towel.

"I'm perfectly fine," I shouted.

When I got out of the shower and wiped steam from the mirror, there was another knock, but this time it wasn't George. It was Rosemary.

"Everything okay?"

Steam hung in the air. I looked at my smoky reflection in the mirror. "I'm fine," I said.

"I'm just checking on you," she said. "Come to my room later, Sequoyah."

At the sound of my name I felt strangely, wildly moved.

BEFORE MY MOTHER WAS locked up, the thought of being kidnapped intrigued me, and there was even a time when I lay in bed some nights, wanting someone to break into our house and take me. The thought never terrified me. Kidnappers were murderers in disguise, I knew this, yet my own kidnapper would be different. My own kidnapper would be some old person drugged on prescription painkillers, too weak or sad to really hurt me. Someone whose idea of comfort meant sitting in silence, staring at an old black-and-white movie on TV. I would be force-fed and not allowed to talk. I would have to watch my kidnapper sleep in a recliner while it rained outside. We would be far away from any city, in a rural area, just the two of us, but it wouldn't be sexual or weird in any way. I would be allowed to walk around the house as I pleased. I would never be bound by rope or tied to any structure. At times he would let me hurt him, hit him with an object, just enough to bruise or draw blood. He would like being treated this way. The environment would feel dangerous only when I considered the police showing up to arrest my kidnapper, drawing their weapons and breaking down the door.

I became obsessed with this thought for a long time.

I'M NOT SURE WHEN, exactly, I became so preoccupied with Rosemary, but I learned more and more about her. I knew she usually wore her hair loose, with bangs, but sometimes she wore it in a ponytail, or back with a hair clip, depending on where she was going. I knew she liked to wear skirts. She liked her black boots. At the same time she could wear a sweater and look more studious. She maintained a mystery about her looks that I found intriguing.

I kept feeling guilty about not accepting her apology. I wasn't sure why it kept bothering me so much. After everyone was asleep I went and knocked lightly on her door. When she opened it I held up two cigarettes.

We sat on the floor by her window, smoking. Outside, I could see the blue parts of the night sky and dirty clouds above what I imagined was Snake River in the distance.

"You're really sensitive, I can tell," she said.

"It isn't a big deal."

"But it's not a bad thing." She tried to explain that it was all a matter of dreams. My dreams reflected the things I worried about, all my fears and anxieties, while at the same time they could provide hope.

"You're really spiritual," she said. "I told you, I can sense that about you. It's not a bad thing."

She allowed me to approach her without fear. She let me place my hands in hers. I'd discovered a frightening, dark world in her room that was unlike any other place I'd been. She tried to explain that everything I was afraid of was a matter of dreams. I told her about my dreams of my mother and father. I told her I was willing to do anything for her, and that I trusted her like a sister even though I'd never had a sister.

Outside, the stray dog started howling. It was a hound of some sort, she told me. A stray from somewhere, probably a farm. The dog barked and howled all the time at night.

"That fucking dog," she said.

On the table beside her bed I saw a photo of her sitting on the grass with another girl, maybe a park somewhere. They were both wearing shorts and looked happy. When I asked her about it she changed the subject.

"So what has Harold told you?" she asked.

"About what?"

"Anything. Have you talked to him much?"

"No, not really."

"And do you know any secrets?"

"About you?"

"Would you even tell me?"

"I'd tell you if I knew anything," I said. I wasn't sure what she was trying to get out of me, so I rested my head in her lap. We both fell silent, and I could feel her hand on the back of my head. We were like this for a while, in the dim, quiet room.

"Everything's going to be okay," she told me, but I knew it wouldn't be.

We could hear the stray dog howling outside.

I SOMETIMES THOUGHT OF Rosemary emerging from the grave as if in some horror film, twitching and laughing, approaching me so that we could search each other's faces and bodies.

"I was thinking we could be twins," I told her one night.

"What do you mean?"

"We look alike, don't you think? I mean if I grew my hair longer. I mean our eyes are similar when we smile."

"I don't know what that means, Sequoyah."

"Maybe I could look more like you if I tried harder."

She had to think about this.

"All I'm saying is we look alike," I said.

Despite her reluctance to admit how alike we were, one afternoon when no one was home she invited me into the bath with her. She had the tub full of bubbles. I pulled off my shirt and got into the tub, still wearing my jeans. The air felt heavy in the warm water. I felt slightly drunk from the moment.

"Weirdo," she said, splashing me.

"Don't get water in my eyes," I said.

"Take a bath like a man," she said.

We spoke slowly, awkwardly. My words felt drunk as I spoke them. They hung there in the room like steam in the heavy air. The water trembled around me. I closed my eyes, and when I opened them she was staring at me.

"We're in the tub," I said.

"Yeah."

"I'm starting to freeze."

She pulled the drain, then got out and put a towel around her. I stood from the tub, watching her as she left the room.

Later she wrote tiny words in French and Spanish in ink on my arms. I didn't want to wash them off. I wanted them drilled into my arm, like a tattoo.

"You should be a tattoo artist," I told her.

"But they aren't my words."

"Drill your art into my body. Your naked people. Your deranged shapes and figures."

"Tribal art for you."

"I want to give you my body when I die," I said.

I sat on her bed and let her smear lipstick on my mouth. She pulled off my shirt and poked around on my chest. She touched my face where my burns are. She let me wear one of her nightgowns. I had on boots and stomped around the room. We smoked cigarettes and listened to Lou Reed.

"Maybe we are alike," she said.

At school the next day, a boy named Simeon Luxe told me he wrote a play about Rosemary called *The Lightning Crash*, because he was secretly in love with her. He said he spent weeks writing it, thinking about her, dreaming they would one day be together.

"Are you jealous?" he asked me.

"Jealous of what?"

"That I'm in love with her."

"No."

"Good," he said. "I wasn't sure if you liked her or what."

He told me his play was about a boy struck by lightning who develops a special superhuman body glow in the night that sparks the attention and interest of a certain girl named Mary Rose. Simeon Luxe wore turtleneck sweaters and colorful threaded bracelets on both wrists. He listened to bands like X and The Damned on his Walkman and told me he could play a guitar solo, note for note, with his teeth.

"I've never actually talked to her," he said, "but I'd give anything to go out with her. Tell her I play the guitar. Or tell her I play drums in a band. Tell her I can play guitar like Keith Richards. I practice in front of the mirror, moving like him. Tell her Slash. Tell her Hendrix."

"I'm not sure," I told him.

"Don't be a goddamn queer," he said. "You got it?"

"Whatever," I said, walking away. I was angry he'd told me all of this, so I never said anything to Rosemary about Simeon Luxe, dumb Simeon Luxe, who later died on October 13, 1999 of mysterious causes.

I have had some time to reflect on those late night confessions when Rosemary was most vulnerable to self-pity, and I was able to witness the honesty in those confessions—one in particular in which she was comfortable enough with me resting my head in her lap. Out of the blue she admitted that, before coming to live with the Troutts, she had attempted suicide, twice.

"Tell me what happened," I said. "How did you do it? You tried to kill yourself. You wanted to be dead."

"Yeah."

"How did you do it?"

She took a cigarette from the pack and lit it, then looked to the window, where a luminous half-moon appeared in the dark sky. I felt a chill in the air—not from the room temperature, but from my own nerves. As I think back on it, I'm sure she could see the look of anticipation in my eyes.

"The first time I took a bunch of pills," she said. "They found me on the floor and rushed me to the hospital. I was sick for a while and on suicide watch at the shelter."

"What kind of pills?"

"Benzos. I wanted to go to sleep and not wake up."

"What about the second time?"

"Um, that's a different story," she said. She showed me the scars on her arm and wrist where she had slashed herself with a knife.

"I don't want to tell you about it," she said.

She lowered the blinds, but a beam of moonlight still slanted through.

"My dad was really good at disappearing," she told me. "He would be in one place and then instantly in another. As I read in bed at night he'd come in to tell me to turn the lamp off, and when I'd look up he would be gone. He helped coach my second grade soccer league one year. I quit after the first game when he didn't show up. Something came up, that was his excuse. My mom told me not to worry about it, but I knew he was secretly relieved that I'd quit. There really weren't many things he liked to do except go hunting. Sometimes I watched him clean his shotgun or feed the baby quail he kept in a big pen in the backyard. He would let me hold the birds. They were tiny and fragile, their heads jerking, too little to fly. I considered them pets and told my class all about them, how they hopped around in their pen and gathered like mice, and that someday I would train them to fly around in my bedroom and bring me my dresses just like in *Cinderella*. But it wasn't like that at all. My dad raised them. He wanted to set them free to hunt."

"It bothered you?"

"I asked him why he had to kill them, and he said for the sport. He drank coffee from a thermos on cold winter mornings before he went hunting at dawn. I would wake up and look out my window to see him carrying his shotgun to his pickup. He wore his camouflage hunting clothes and a hat. I tried to think about him out in the fields with his friends, trudging through brush or creeks in pursuit of deer or quail, how the sudden blast of the shotgun must've sent so many birds scattering from trees. I once saw a dead deer with its belly sliced open. My dad's friend showed it to us in the barn behind his house. The deer's hooves were tied as it hung upside down, its belly cut open and dripping with blood. It was one of the saddest fucking things I've ever seen."

When I got into bed later, I looked over and saw George asleep, snoring with his mouth open. I hadn't heard him snore before, and it took a while for me to fall asleep. Sometime in the middle of the night I woke to his hand on my brow. It frightened me at first. I told him to go back to bed. He insisted on brushing my hair with his hand despite my telling him to stop. I pushed his hand away and told him, again, to go to bed. He never spoke, but eventually he stopped when I sat up and squeezed his hand.

"Go to bed," I said.

The next day he claimed he didn't remember, blaming it on sleepwalking. "I've walked downstairs all the way to the back porch," he told me. "I've walked into the kitchen and turned on the oven. I've walked into the bathroom and pulled on the shower curtain. But it only happens about twice a year."

"It's fine," I said.

Agnes confirmed, saying it's never been a problem. "I've only seen it happen once. He was trying to get into Rosemary's room, but the door was locked. That was last year sometime. I just led him back to bed and it was fine."

When Agnes left the room, I followed George outside to the shed. The sun was still out, but it had gotten colder. I helped George open the shed door, which required a lot of force as it tended to stick. I'd never been in this shed before, had never had a reason to go inside. George pulled the chain for the light, and I thought it looked like any other shed: full of tools, a garden hose, those sorts of things. The light bulb swung over our heads.

"I need to show you this," George said, walking to the corner. There was plywood and two-by-fours stacked against the wall. The shed was a dark, lively place full of a sawdust smell.

The floor of the shed was made of bricks. George knelt down and removed two of the bricks and pulled out a brown paper sack. He opened it, looked inside, then motioned for me to come over and look.

"What is it?" I asked.

"Come see."

I was expecting a dead animal or something. A rat, a rabbit's foot, something grotesque and strange, maybe some artifact George was hiding from everyone else.

When I looked inside the sack, though, I saw money. One hundred dollar bills wrapped in rubber bands. The sack was full of them. I'd never seen so much money in my life.

"Holy shit," I said. "How much money is here? Is this yours?"

"It's Harold's," he said.

I reached inside and pulled out a couple of stacks. We emptied the sack and counted ten stacks.

"They're all one hundreds," he said. "In stacks of ten. So that's ten thousand."

"Shit," I said again.

"Last time I checked there was six thousand. I think it changes every week."

I'd heard of people burying large amounts of cash back then. I never knew if it was true, but I did know that people back home didn't trust anyone with their money. They especially didn't trust the banks or the IRS. There was also the matter of avoiding taxes when large amounts of cash were at stake. I'd heard of tribal members doing it on their land. The way I saw it, there was a million dollars probably buried around the state.

"How did you find this?" I asked. "Did he tell you about it?"

"I was in here counting bricks one day. I noticed these were loose, so I pulled one out and noticed the sack."

I put the stacks in my lap. I wanted to hold it, all that money, like it was mine.

"We can't take it," George said. "He'll know we took it. But I wanted to show it to you."

"Ten thousand dollars," I said.

"Yeah."

"Why did you show it to me?"

"You're my friend," he said. "I figured you'd want to see it."

I didn't know what to say. The thought of stealing only one of the hundred dollar bills crossed my mind, but I knew I didn't want to take it. I put it back into the sack, and George stuffed it back into the floor, covering it with the bricks.

Outside, the wind was cold. I waited for George to lock up the shed. The sky was full of dark clouds. A flock of geese flew over our heads, making noise.

MY BEST DAYDREAMS HAPPENED in school, when I thought about my mother and me before we left Cherokee County. There was one time in particular, when we were at a pond on the outskirts of town, just the two of us. We caught a couple of perch and threw them back into the water. The pond was small and we walked around it, casting our reels. My grandpa had taught me how to fish when I was very young, as he had taught my mother and her brothers when they were kids. He'd died young, in his forties, from a heart attack. As my mother and I fished, she told me about how her father had died mowing his lawn. My grandmother found him lying in the grass, the lawnmower still running. He was dead, staring into the ground. My grandmother knelt among a ragged confinement of leaves and grass shavings and touched his cheek. He was a good, hardworking man, my mother told me.

This was probably the only time we ever talked about death.

At school I had trouble concentrating and struggled to keep my eyes open. I thought about my mother sitting tense in prison, sleeping on a concrete bed, curled up under a small gray blanket. Or sitting on the floor of her cell, stricken with guilt, crying as she thought of me. I thought of the days she took me to the library when I was very young. I thought of sitting on her lap while she read to me until I fell asleep to her voice. I fell asleep in Oklahoma History class and woke to the clanging bell, my head on my desk. People were rushing out of the room.

In the third floor bathroom I saw Mr. Gillis standing by the far wall.

"Hello, Sequoyah," he said.

I went to the urinal and relieved myself. Mr. Gillis was making clicking noises with his tongue. When I finished I went to the sink and turned on the water. I leaned in close to the mirror and examined the redness on my cheek from where my head had been resting on the desk while I slept in class. We heard the siren of a police car from somewhere outside. We both looked out the window for a moment.

"Do you happen to know a student named Marissa Flores, by chance?" he asked. "She's a sophomore on the pep squad."

"Sorry, I don't think so."

"Medium-length brown hair?"

"Sorry."

"It's nothing," he said. "Forget it. I'm just taking a break here. I tend to get lonely during the day, thinking about my life. I miss my house. I miss the living room, with the Oriental rug I bought in Santa Cruz. I miss the mauve curtains. I miss the bedroom, with its updated light fixtures and wallpaper. I miss the dining room, the cherrywood and oak table. I miss the bathroom, with the tub, where my ex-wife smoked Virginia Slims while I sat on the floor beside her."

"I should head back to class," I said without looking at him.

"Who knows where she is," he mumbled. He slouched into the wall.

In the last class of the day, I stared bored out the window. It was cloudless and dead outside. I saw the desolate street leading into the old downtown of Little Crow. I saw branches of trees, cars parked along the curb. I saw a delivery truck stop in the middle of the street, its taillights flashing. The light from the window moved at various angles, which made me sleepy. I thought of an old neighbor, Paolo Valensi, a local artist, who lived next door to my mother and me when we were in Cherokee County. Paolo found himself in such a deep depression that he could no longer paint. "Nothing comes alive on canvas," Paolo told my mother. Paolo struggled with his own personal demons, having developed a reputation for being moody, drunk, and a little crazy. He had never married, and his loneliness caused an emptiness and decline in his work. Most nights he spent in the town pub, getting drunk. I wondered what happened to Paolo.

I was given detention for sleeping so much in class. I had to call Agnes and lie that I was staying late for extra help in math. Agnes told me to walk downtown to the thrift store where Rosemary was working and she would bring me home. In detention I sat in a classroom with three other boys, all of us with our heads down. The teacher at the desk was a coach of some sort, wearing a warm-up suit and sneakers. He was reading the paper. A girl came in late and sat by the window. She pulled out a notebook and started doing homework. The teacher kept reading the newspaper. He never said anything until it was time to go.

When detention ended I slung my backpack over my shoulder and walked a few blocks toward downtown. It wasn't too cold out, though there was a chill in the air and the sky looked like a frozen lake. Outside Edson's Pharmacy, an older man wearing a hat and sunglasses was sitting in a chair with a small dog at his feet. The dog was a black-and-white bulldog with a pug nose.

"Hello," the man said when he noticed I was looking at the dog. Though I couldn't see his eyes, up close I noticed he had mostly gray hair. He was smiling behind sunglasses. "You can pet him if you want. He doesn't bite."

I leaned down and scratched the dog behind the ears. The dog was panting.

"What's your name?" the man asked.

"Sequoyah," I said, still petting the dog.

"I'm Jack," he said. "This is Bo. He likes you, Sequoyah."

I stood back up, and Jack asked if I had a dog of my own.

"No, we had a dog when I was little but it ran off. My mom thinks he got run over."

"Oh my, that's sad," Jack said. "What was his name? Was it a boy?"

"Girl. Her name was Sabine. She was a Lab."

"I bet she was sweet, Sequoyah. How old are you?"

"Fifteen."

"Where are you headed?"

"Thrift store for my ride home. I better go."

"All right," he said. "See you later, Sequoyah." He was still smiling.

I walked past the dark windows of downtown stores, past the barber shop and travel agency, where a woman was standing out front, smoking a cigarette and looking at her nails, bored. She caught my eye as I walked past. Half a block down I made it to the thrift store, finally, where I saw Rosemary through the front window. I stood outside a moment and watched her. She was standing at the register, talking to her friend, Nora Drake. A moment later she looked up and saw me. I opened the door and a bell chimed.

"Hey," she said. "I'm not off work just yet. There's still like fifteen minutes if you want to wait outside. Cool?"

Nora was looking at me like I'd interrupted something important.

"Okay," I said, and went back out.

I sat on the curb and smoked a cigarette. A man carrying a briefcase walked to his car and looked at me in disdain. He kept watching me, even after he got into his car and pulled away. When Rosemary and Nora came out, they were still engaged in conversation. I stood and she told Nora she would call her later. Nora never said anything to me. She never even looked at me.

In the car, as we pulled out of the lot, I told Rosemary about Jack, the man with the dog, and asked if she'd ever met him before.

"There he is," I said, pointing to him. He was still sitting in front of Edson's Pharmacy with his dog.

"I don't know him," she said. "I've never even seen him before."

ONE TIME I SAW Jack at the supermarket, but he wasn't wearing his hat, and he didn't have his dog. I was grocery shopping with Agnes and George, pushing the cart for Agnes, when I saw him in the breakfast cereal aisle, reading the label on a box of cereal. He saw me, and I knew he recognized me, because he gave an abrupt smile, but I kept pushing the cart.

While we were in the checkout line, George flipped through a magazine. I kept looking around to make sure Jack wasn't following us.

At school I kept hearing stories about Rosemary. Late in the night certain teenage boys and some of the girls from school engaged in strange sex acts and witchcraft. Rosemary's name was brought up during these stories. I heard of similar adult sex parties, where people dressed like mannequins. Some of the women wore wigs or hair extensions, and they all wore flesh-colored bodysuits.

Even backyard birthday parties involved a game in which children were blindfolded and had their wrists tied behind their backs. They bobbed for dead snakes from a tub of water.

"I went to one of those parties last year," George later told me. "One of my friends from school has parents who are supposedly in some sort of religious cult. I'm not sure if it's true or not, but at my friend's younger brother's birthday party we were invited to bob for real dead snakes. I saw them."

"Did you do it?" I asked.

"No, but my friend did."

"What kind of snakes were they?"

"I don't know," he said. "I think the ones they used in church."

Around town, many women had long dark hair and wore ankle-length dresses, and I always wondered if they were trying to look like Rosemary. It wasn't a radical thought. The local beauty shop downtown started giving a 40 percent discount on all hair extensions, so that when women walked out their hair hung down past their shoulders. Husbands bought long dresses and threw away their wives' makeup. George told me that Ed Krim, the retired school superintendent, brought his wife to the beauty shop for their golden anniversary. She wanted a makeover. Mrs. Krim was seventy-three and used a walker to get around. In the "Around Town" section of the newspaper, a picture showed a beautician posing with her hands in Mrs. Krim's hair while Mr. Krim watched in horror from the shadows.

Even Agnes wore her hair long, though it was often up. I asked George why she did this. Was it a coincidence that all the other women in town were doing the same? Why did the entire town seem to have the same strange habits? The question made him think for a long time.

"Little Crow is just a really weird place," he said. "The police promote prostitution. There's a brothel out by the lake. The police know all about it and they don't care."

"The police promote prostitution?"

"They're so crooked," he said. "Don't look so surprised. It's this town. You'll see. You could probably get away with murder here."

• • •

THE NEXT DAY AT school was the same old thing. I tried to stay awake, but my boredom left me preoccupied with hurting myself in the classroom, in front of everyone. *Look, look, look*, I would say. *Look: I punctured my skin with my ink pen. Look: I stabbed myself with a knife.* I could slice my thumb or my arm. Everyone would watch the blood ooze out and spread across the desk. I thought of the color red, and blood, and the slimy organs in my body, and the parts of my body that were covered with clothes. I thought of my body as a disfigurement, with putrid flesh, the skin underneath my shirt stretched and molded into a deformation.

"The five civilized tribes," Mrs. Speck was saying.

Mrs. Speck stood in front of the class wearing a skirt and black knee-high socks. Mrs. Speck was an older, homely woman who was rumored to hide vodka in her desk and drink whenever she smoked in the teachers' lounge on her free period. She talked about Oklahoma's history, the Dust Bowl, winds sweeping across the plains bringing giant billows of dirt like smoke, a plague of jackrabbits invading fields and pastures. I imagined myself suddenly standing on my desk and shouting curse words. I imagined Mrs. Speck removing her blouse and unfastening her bra, freeing her sagging breasts. Mrs. Speck, a large, lonely woman in need of attention from boys. They would rush to her. They would play with her breasts while she drank vodka from a flask. The girls would run out of the classroom in horror.

"The Creeks," Mrs. Speck said. "The Choctaws, the Seminoles."

Someone could've held the class hostage. Someone could've walked into the school and started firing a gun, though such things were rare in the late 1980s. In 1989 we had no school security officers, no police patrol, no metal detectors. There were no drug dogs or locker checks or gun fears. I imagined some psychopath walking into the school and pointing a military semi-automatic assault rifle at the class, ordering us all to get on the floor. He would walk slowly around the room, all crazy-eyed and spitting as he yelled at us. I thought of the sounds of classmates crying out while the psychopath tied Mrs. Speck to her chair. And what would he do then? Because just shooting everyone wouldn't be enough, not for him or for the media. Because he would execute Mrs. Speck and force us to watch, shooting her in the head. Because he would then turn the rifle on himself and shoot himself in the head so that the effect would be an entire bloodbath splattered around the room.

"Periodic warfare," Mrs. Speck said.

At the end of the day I sat in detention while the dumpy teacher sat reading his newspaper. Everyone was so quiet you could hear someone's stomach growling in the room. This time more students were there, including an older boy who scribbled zigzag lines on his desk with a pen the entire time. He saw me watching him and leaned over and asked me in a whisper if I smoked pot.

"Sometimes," I whispered back. "You got some?"

"I know where some is," he whispered.

"No talking," the teacher said from behind his newspaper.

After detention ended, the boy told me his name was Jamie. He asked if I knew Horace Prairiewolf.

"No," I said. "Who's Horace Prairiewolf?"

"He's got some weed," Jamie said. "He lives in that house on the corner."

Five minutes later we were standing on Horace's porch while Jamie beat on the door with his fist. When Horace opened the door I saw a large man, maybe in his thirties, standing nearly seven feet, with long dark hair that partly covered his face. He looked vicious. He was shirtless and dark-skinned and wearing blue jeans. I wondered if he'd been asleep. Horace looked me over. "This your cousin?" he asked Jamie.

"No, just a kid from school."

"I'm Horace," he said. He studied me for a minute then invited us in. His house was small and dark and warm. A ceiling fan hummed in the living room. We followed Horace into the small kitchen, where he pulled on a T-shirt and said he had porcupine meat in his freezer. "Also deer and bobcat meat," he said. "You guys hungry?"

"I'm not," Jamie said. "We were just wanting to see if you had any weed."

"Porcupine liver is good," he said. "I can clean it if you ever bring it to me."

Jamie looked at me, then back at Horace.

"Venison roast is good, too," Horace said. He told us deer meat is healthy to eat, low in fat and high in protein, with natural salts. He said he'd killed a deer with his bare hands. He said he shot a hawk and ripped out its guts.

"I do it to keep living," he said. "People who are dying are desperate, my friends."

"You're dying?" Jamie said.

"I need medicine."

We sat in his living room watching him roll a joint. He lit it and handed it to Jamie, who took a long drag. Jamie handed me the joint and I took a drag, holding the smoke in my lungs. I'd smoked before and knew I could get high easily.

"Pretty good weed," Jamie said.

"I didn't put much in when I rolled it," Horace said. "Take another hit."

I took one more drag, then handed it back to Horace.

We watched TV for a while. An old western movie showed a cowboy in a saloon. The cowboy knocked back a shot of whiskey and kicked over a spittoon. Another cowboy came up to him from behind and beat him over the head with a chair, shattering it. Then the two cowboys started fistfighting.

"Muskrat and bobcat is good," Horace said. "You like meat, you'll like it. Deer meat is good. Brown the loin in a skillet. Braise the shoulder and neck. Put it in a pot and make a good stew."

"My grandma makes stew," Jamie said.

"Meat is undercooked, you get sick," Horace said. "The muskrat had roundworms. Shit, it made Otto sick as a dog."

I yawned and realized the sun was going down outside. I'd stayed too long. Agnes would be waiting for me.

"My ride," I said, "Shit, I forgot about it."

"I'm staying," Jamie said.

"Be good, brother," Horace called out.

I left and ran down the street back to the school, where I saw Agnes's car and a police car waiting. My heart was racing. I thought I'd blown everything and that the police would take me back to Liz and I'd have to go back to a shelter somewhere. I felt sick to my stomach at the thought of it. Throughout my life, I've always had a sense of distorted reality whenever panic sets in—time seems to suspend and colors and shapes become more vivid. As I approached Agnes, who had gotten out of the car and was talking to the police officer beside her, I felt as though everything around me had intensified in color and sound: the rustle of trees lining the street, the blinding blue of the sky, the leaves tumbling across the school lawn. They both saw me coming and were talking, but I couldn't hear what they were saying. When I reached them the first thing I did was apologize.

"Sorry, I didn't realize it was this late," I said.

"I waited for thirty minutes," Agnes said. "Where were you?"

"I walked to a friend's house and lost track of time."

"I waited thirty minutes," she said again. "I went inside the school and they told me you'd left. So I had to call Liz and she told me to call the police."

My throat felt swollen. Agnes apologized to the police officer, who told her it wasn't a big deal. "The important thing is that he's okay," he said, then turned to me. "Your social worker is worried," he said.

Agnes said we would call her the minute we got home. Suddenly I felt relieved. I was worried they could smell the pot on me, but the wind must've helped cover the smell. I didn't want to go back to a shelter and start taking drug tests.

"It's always important to be aware of the time," the officer told me, whatever that meant.

"Yes, sir," I said.

Agnes apologized and the officer got into his patrol car and pulled away.

"You'll need to call Liz when we get home," Agnes said as we got into the car.

I apologized again and she fell silent. We drove through downtown. I saw the man in the hat sitting in front of the pharmacy with his dog. As we drove by he saw me and waved. I didn't wave back. We drove east out of town in silence, past the refinery and older vacant buildings, heading for the countryside.

"I'm just thinking," Agnes finally said, "you need to be careful about friends."

"I know," I said.

"I think maybe you're easily manipulated," she said.

Agnes was right—I was always easily influenced. A couple of years before going to live at the Troutts, I'd spent a weekend in juvenile detention. My friend Coco and I got caught with weed when we were walking through the park. He'd talked me into going with him to get a baggie and some rolling papers from a friend of his older brother. Coco had a part-time job so he always had money. For a while he bought our cigarettes from the cigarette vending machine at the bowling alley. In the park, on a Friday night, the police caught us, handcuffed us and drove us to the detention center. Coco and I were both lucky to get released the following Monday with juvenile probation and fifty hours community service, which I did that summer at the public library.

As I recall, the detention center was very different from any shelter. The staff graded you with points based on your behavior, and if you really screwed up they immediately dropped you to level four. The higher the level meant the more privileges you got, like getting to stay up later and getting an extra snack and getting to play ping-pong. Level fours didn't get a snack and went to bed at eight.

Everybody there looked basically the same since we were all wearing green jumpsuits. Most of the residents were boys. My first night there I got in trouble for sitting down before being told to, and as punishment I had to sit in a chair facing the wall for ten minutes. It was very military-like, really strict. You couldn't look around or talk or even move your hands without the staff thinking you were giving gang signs. And ten minutes lasts an eternity when you're facing a wall.

Luckily, I'd managed not to get in any more trouble for

the rest of the weekend. At one point we were instructed to line up at the door to go outside for our daily group exercises. Three guards accompanied us outside. Two stood at the corners of the fence, and the third walked around, making sure everyone was doing what they were supposed to. We did exercises—jumping jacks, sit-ups, leg lifts, butterfly kicks. The outside court was surrounded by a tall fence, probably twelve or thirteen feet high. I wondered if anyone had ever tried to make a run for it. There wasn't barbed wire on the fence, but the guards were positioned and appeared ready for anything. I couldn't imagine anyone trying to escape out there.

We did about thirty minutes of exercises, then got to rest while the staff set up the volleyball net. Outside was the only time you could whisper to someone without the staff catching you. The kid who was beside me tried talking to me. I didn't know who he was. I didn't even look at him. While watching the guards set up the net, he whispered, "Hey, what happened?"

"Shut up," I said, shielding my face with my hand.

"I hate this fucking place," he whispered.

I paused for a moment, since one of the guards was looking in our direction. He looked away. After the guards positioned the volleyball poles, they divided us into teams and we played volleyball until it was time to go in. The boy didn't try whispering to me anymore. I didn't want to get into trouble, I just wanted to go back to my room and wait for court on Monday. We lined up against the wall again, and one of the guards led everyone inside while the other two followed behind us. It did cross my mind to turn and make a run for it. If I didn't think I had a chance of going home at court, I really might've tried it.

Later that day, in the bathroom, I ran cold water on my face and looked at myself in the mirror. A moment later I heard a knock on the door. It was one of the male guards telling me to hurry up.

"Give me a minute," I said, and touched my face against the mirror, but he kept knocking. Finally I opened the door, and he was standing there with his arms crossed, yelling at me that I'd taken too long. I told him I didn't realize I'd taken that long.

"Don't backtalk me," he said. "How would I know you weren't trying to hurt yourself? Get over here and give me twenty push-ups."

I got down and, very slowly, managed to do maybe five or six push-ups, but that was all. I really tried. I stayed down there on my hands and knees since he didn't tell me to get up.

"Stay there," he said. "You'll like being on your knees once you're in prison."

That's the way it was there, a place full of guys who liked to bully kids. It was way worse than any shelter.

GEORGE BUSIED HIMSELF WITH writing at night, in our room, telling me he was becoming more and more observant of his surroundings. There were all sorts of strange people living in Little Crow, he said. There were drug addicts and deranged derelicts and farmers who raised wild animals. There were sick criminals and gamblers and religious cult members. People slept homeless in the streets while others lived in grand homes. He finished off his beef stew as he sat on his bed then set the empty bowl on the nightstand beside him.

"I'm working hard on my novel," he kept saying, looking over at me and waiting with new hope for some sort of reaction.

"You want to read me some of it?" I asked.

"Not really. I can't read it aloud to you. I hope you understand. I wanted to tell you that my mom kept talking about my dad after he died. She started drinking."

"Mine too," I said.

He had to think about this. "Your dad died?"

"No, he left. But my mom started drinking, too.

He was flipping through his novel manuscript pages. "All right," he said, "I'll read a short section of my book. You still want to hear it?"

"Sure."

He took a minute before he started to read:

"There are many men from our town who were executed for doing horrible things. Jimmy Lowry and Elmer Pigmel headed east on Highway 66 to the little town of Agnew to rob the First National Bank on Main Street. They ate at a small café down the street from the bank beforehand. Jimmy stayed in the car while Elmer went inside and pointed the .45 at the teller. 'No vault,' he told her. 'Just the drawers.' The teller emptied the drawers and he stuffed the bills into a paper sack and then ran out as the

alarm was going off. They made it fifteen miles outside of town before the police caught up with them."

He stopped reading and looked up to see my reaction.

"I thought it was a science fiction novel?" I asked.

"This is early in the novel," he said. "It's going to be a big book. I want to write big books. Do you want to hear more?"

"Yeah, sure."

"Paul Laffenfly," he continued, *"a sixth grade teacher at Jefferson Middle School, went berserk one afternoon when his students wouldn't cooperate. It happened near the end of the school year, when the weather outside was warm and bright and the students were restless. Paul screamed at his students, who laughed at him. He wrestled a student to the floor of the classroom and hog-tied him with rope he kept, for whatever reason, in the bottom drawer of his desk. Also executed that year was Officer Plummet, who was charged with involuntary manslaughter and second degree murder for the death of a mentally ill homeless man who was looking in the windows of parked cars. Officer Plummet claimed the homeless man had raised his arms in a gesture of threat, which caused Plummet to fire his weapon and shoot the man in the chest three times. Officers Gaines, Stolp, and Ricks were all involved. They were held in the county jail but were later released on bond. They eventually confessed to helping Plummet with the murder by holding the mentally ill man down before Plummet shot him. They were executed the following October."*

He looked at me again, and this time I nodded to let him know I was listening. He continued: *"Last October, Archie Moon was executed for indecent exposure and performing lewd acts in public at the M.E. Griffin Nursing Home. Moon, who had been a staff member for over fifteen years, was working the night shift on a blustery winter night in January. After residents went to bed, Moon removed all his clothes and entered the rooms of Eleanor Eldenhurst, Marjorie Peele, and Ethel Wurth respectively, waking them and forcing them to watch him as he held his genitals and grunted. All three women had difficulty describing the specific details. Pastor Hughes continues to meet with them once a month for counseling and support."*

He stopped reading there.

"Where's the bloodbath," I said. "The wives should lose it and start killing everyone."

He sort of shrugged.

"Weird stuff. Maybe you'll get rich."

He didn't seem pleased. I didn't know what else to say. He wouldn't read any more.

"I'm going to bed," he said. He turned off his lamp and rolled over in bed.

"Hey," I said. "What the hell? What's the problem?"

He didn't answer.

THAT NIGHT, IN SLEEP, I dreamed a band of outlaws buried my father somewhere in Mexico, but he returned from the dead. In the dream I was sitting on a bench in the park with my old friends Coco and White Eagle when I saw him standing by a tree.

"We're going to Hollywood," White Eagle said. "That man over there is taking us to Hollywood."

"What man? I asked. "The one by the tree?"

"Ask Coco," White Eagle said. "He'll tell you all about it."

Coco was looking at his nails and humming.

"What man?" I asked Coco.

I looked at my father standing by the tree. He was polishing his trumpet, about to play. He had a long, white beard. He was dressed in an expensive suit.

"What man?" I kept asking.

Some kids were climbing on the monkey bars nearby. One of the boys was chasing another boy. A woman, maybe their mother, sat on a bench watching them. Next to the tree, my father started playing his trumpet.

"I'm leaving," I said to Coco and White Eagle.

"Wait, don't leave us," they said. "Don't go now. We're going to Hollywood, right?"

But I stood and walked over to my father and didn't look back at anyone.

When my father saw me, he stopped playing his trumpet and looked at me as if he recognized me. I saw dirt and grass and bits of twigs in his hair. I saw tiny worms on his clothes and in his ears. His hands were dry and cracked and bloody.

In my dream I knew he had returned from the dead. They had buried my father, but he returned to me.

"It's a sad dream," Rosemary later told me. "I understand you."

We were in her room. It was late, and Rosemary liked to

keep her room dim, lit only by a small lamp. Her curtains had a floral pattern but she'd marked all over them in black marker, scribbled shapes, drawings of arrows and ears and tongues. I hadn't noticed it before, and when I asked her about it she waved it off.

"It doesn't mean anything," she said.

I lit a cigarette and watched her on the bed. She brought her knees to her chest, and her hair fell over part of her face.

"I had a lover last year," she said, "but only briefly. Harold and Agnes had no idea. She was older. She was really beautiful. She told me she was a traveler. We talked about living in Paris. She'd climbed rocks in Ontario, hiked in the Chiricahuas. I would sneak her in at night after they went to bed."

"How old was she?"

"Thirty. She was from Ecuador."

"I thought you liked guys."

"I do."

"In a sexual way?" I said this quickly, maybe too quickly, so that it came out sounding meaner than I intended.

"Trust me, I like boys," she said. "Last year I met this Greek guy at a party by the lake. The next day he came to my work and picked me up on his motorcycle. He took me to his place and we fucked for two hours."

I wanted to hear more.

"He undressed me," she said. "He tied my wrists behind my back and forced me to the floor. I didn't mind, though.

I watched him sit in the corner and reveal himself. I waited for him to come over to me. I yelled for him to come to me."

She hooked a strand of hair behind her ear and looked at me. She was trying to see my reaction. I think she was surprised I didn't seem shocked, which made me question whether she was telling the truth.

"We fucked for two hours," she said.

"You already said that."

"You think I'm lying."

"No, I believe you."

"You look like you don't," she said. "He crawled out of the room while I got dressed. He crawled to his shoes. He couldn't walk."

"What happened to your lover, the woman from Ecuador?"

"All that matters is that I like older women. I like to be touched by a woman, which is better."

"Like Nora," I said.

"Funny you bring her up. She fucking hates you."

In the days that followed I felt as though my hatred for Nora Drake only grew worse. My hatred for the way she talked to me. My hatred for her overall demeanor as it related to everyone else in our house. And my hatred for life when I was around her, and how I thought about death, other people dying, the death of my mother and father, Rosemary, even George. To think of Nora Drake years later in this way is to think of resurrection, a body rising from the earth, covered in dirt and bugs and sickness.

For a while, right after my mother was locked up, Liz had me seeing a counselor every week after school. Her name was Karen and she was a soft-spoken woman in her forties, I guessed. I had been in Karen's office so many times that I had her body language down. I knew that by nodding she was comforting me. I knew that when she leaned back to cross her legs and spread her hands over her skirt she was about to offer a suggestion, which was usually followed by her removing her glasses and putting the handle in her mouth to await my reaction. From the beginning, after recognizing these things,

I could tell that she would try to make me aware of my problems. She did this by basically repeating whatever I'd just said, which I figured out early on was probably a tactic to reassure me that she was listening. I didn't mind, though.

Karen and I had already been through all the drama of me dealing with my mother being locked up, and also my loneliness issues, and there were times when I opened up completely and told her how I sometimes felt manipulative, like the time when I'd stolen my aunt Desi's Godiva chocolates and ate them, then ran upstairs and smeared the chocolate from my fingers all over my cousin's bedroom door so she'd think he did it. Desi was a firm disciplinarian and spanked him, and I curled up in my bed and listened to my Walkman to avoid hearing him cry. I didn't really care, though. Karen listened silently to everything I had to say. Then, out of nowhere, things just stopped working. I had nothing to say and felt compelled to make conversation: our conversations were always forced and awkward, consisting of me saying things that made her lean forward and nod a great deal and give lots of praise, which seemed overly dramatic and hollow, as if she liked to make a big production out of nothing.

One time she asked me if I ever felt like harming myself or anyone else, and I lied and said I didn't. But the truth was that I wanted to harm lots of people, especially the other kids at school who laughed when a teacher called on me because I wasn't paying attention. Soon enough I felt the counseling wasn't helping. I always liked Karen, but things weren't getting any better, and she never gave real answers, only her usual replies: "What's most important is how you *feel* about it, Sequoyah. How do you *feel* about that?" and so forth. I looked to her for peace and came away with nothing. During our last visit, I told her I was angry and hurting, and that I wanted answers about my mother being locked up. Everything seemed unfair.

"I understand," she said. "But you'll have to give it time."

She told me that if I were to cup my hands in water and squeeze, then the water would run through my fingers and be gone. "Do you understand what I'm saying?" she asked.

"I guess so," I said. "But how can I not miss her?"

After that last visit, I left with the hope that I would be able to put everything in the past—all those horrible nights I'd had and the dreadful days that would try to haunt me in the future. I walked away without ever wanting to return.

But I hadn't been angry at anyone in a long time until Nora started coming around. I continued to see her at the house, and she and Rosemary spent time in Rosemary's room with the door closed. Whenever Nora saw me she gave me a look like she detested me for some reason. I'd never even had a conversation with her, yet she despised me.

Then, on a Saturday afternoon when I was sitting with George at the kitchen table, she came up to me and asked if I would accompany her and Rosemary to a spot near the lake. Her pet rabbit had died, she said, and she needed someone to dig a small grave so she could bury him.

"It won't take long," she said in a quiet, low voice. "Do you mind going with us?"

"Where's the rabbit?" I asked.

"In the car. He's in a garbage sack in the trunk."

"It's a nice day outside," Rosemary said. "Can you help us out?"

I agreed, but only because Rosemary asked. I went out to the shed and got a small shovel, then met them at Nora's car in the driveway. She popped the trunk and I saw the garbage sack. I set the small shovel next to it and slammed the trunk closed.

I was sitting in the back seat, alone, when my head started hurting again. Rosemary sat in the passenger's seat directly in front of me. Nora backed out of the driveway and drove us through Little Crow, passing the downtown stores, over the railroad tracks and past the body shop, Whirlwind Cleaners, Green Carpet Motor Lodge. As we turned onto Lakeview Road, I closed my eyes and tried to imagine a row of fluttering colors, pinks and blues, reds and whites. I found doing so was calming and meditative and I hoped it would help my headache, but it didn't. Now and then I opened my eyes to see Rosemary gazing at Nora from behind her sunglasses, and I found myself longing for Rosemary, or anyone, really, to look at me in such a way.

Swiftly we turned off Lakeview Road and drove down a winding dirt road toward the lake. We passed the boathouse and the bait and tackle shop, then pulled into a secluded area surrounded by trees. Across the road the grass was as tall as me.

"My head is hurting," I said.

Rosemary gave me two aspirin, but nobody had any kind of drink so I had to chew the pills up. They were chalky and gross, but I needed something to help.

"Well?" I said to Nora. "Where are we doing this?"

She popped the trunk and we all got out of the car. "You'll need to follow us," she said, looking at me. "Oh, and what's the deal with the eyeliner? Is there something you want to tell us?"

I ignored her. From the trunk I took the small shovel and black garbage sack with the dead rabbit. As I picked it up I felt the rabbit, and I imagined its body inside already turning stiff, its big ears and open eyes. "Do you want me to bury it in the sack?" I asked Nora.

"It doesn't matter. You can keep him in the sack if you don't want to see him. I can't stand to see him dead."

Rosemary shivered in the cold. Though it was sunny, and the sky was a deep blue, the wind blew in chilly bursts. I knew the ground would be hard to dig, even a small hole.

I slammed the trunk and followed them down a dirt path, through the sticky grass, with interlaced branches on both sides of us. We followed the path down a hill as it led to a clearing near the lake, where they stopped walking. Nora was looking around. Rosemary dug in her purse for a cigarette and lit it in the wind. I waited for them to tell me something.

Nora looked at Rosemary. "This is the spot," she said. She

looked at me. "It's really sad. I hope you know. We'll walk down to the lake while you bury him, okay? Come down when you're finished."

"You're not staying?" I asked.

"It's too sad," she said.

Rosemary handed her a cigarette. Nora leaned in close and Rosemary lit it for her. I wanted one, too, but she didn't offer, and I'd forgotten to bring mine.

"All right," I said. "I'll do this then come find you guys."

"Thanks, Sequoyah," Rosemary said. Then they walked away. I watched them head down the path to the lake until they disappeared into the trees. Then I set the box down and started digging in the dirt. The ground was hard from the winter freeze, so it took a little while for me to dig deep enough for a rabbit. When I finished I set the shovel down and picked up the trash sack and opened it. I'm not sure why I wanted to look inside, whether it was some grim curiosity or whether I wanted to make sure Nora was being honest. I felt like maybe this could've been some sort of mean trick she was playing on me, and had dragged Rosemary into it, simply to humiliate me. But when I looked inside there it was, a brown rabbit curled on its side. Its eyes were dark and wide open. I immediately tied the sack and dropped it into the hole, then covered it with all the loose dirt. When I finished I patted it with the shovel. My heart was racing.

I carried the shovel down the path toward the lake to find Rosemary and Nora, but as I made my way through the grass and trees, closer to the water, they were nowhere to be found. I looked off in the distance, where the path led around the lake to a park, and wondered if they might've walked down there.

The view of the lake was blocked by tall weeds off to the side, and the path continued down a slight hill, winding around a large rock. I followed the path without looking back from where I came. It was like being in a dream where you're walking down your neighborhood street on a sunny day, then turn a corner and suddenly you're trudging through a brutal blizzard. I was afraid of looking back in case the scene had changed completely, but somehow I felt better knowing I needed to only pay attention to what was ahead of me.

From the brackish water I smelled dead fish as I walked along the bank, and I kept thinking it was the smell of dead things—dead fish, dead rabbits, maybe another dead animal somewhere. I wondered what a dead person smelled like. I wondered if someone found Nora dead here, would she smell worse than the dead fish? Would she become as rotten as a dead animal, curled up from rigor mortis, with bugs and maggots crawling in her hair and covering her body?

Then I came upon a clearing beside the lake where they were sitting together, Nora resting her head on Rosemary's shoulder. For a moment I stayed back and watched them. I knelt down in the brush. The leaves curled dry at my feet, and a cold air hung around me as I watched. Rosemary picked up a tiny rock and threw it at the water. She turned and said something to Nora, who pointed to the spot where she threw it. I imagined them undressing and walking to the water. I imagined them entering the lake and splashing around until Rosemary became annoyed and accidentally held Nora underwater too long. I thought of the struggle, Rosemary's laugh, then Nora's body floating to the surface, dead. I dug my heels into the hard earth, into the dirty leaves and brush. The lake may as well have been frozen black. They weren't moving or going anywhere. I wanted them to become consumed by anger, consumed by something, but nothing happened.

As I approached, the sky opened up. They both looked at me, and in that moment I felt an emptiness that I hadn't felt in a long time.

I said, "It's done. I buried him."

Nora didn't say anything. She didn't thank me. I looked out toward the lake and started to walk away, my head buzzing from fatigue or something. I stepped down the hill, which was steep, but slipped and fell. When I fell I must've lost consciousness for a moment because I only remember Rosemary kneeling down to console me.

"Your head is bleeding a little," she said.

But nothing brought me in touch with the moment, not seeing Rosemary as she tried to console me, not her hand touching my head, and certainly not Nora Drake, who wasn't even concerned, Nora who hadn't thanked me.

"It's just a scrape," Rosemary said, and helped me sit up. "Nora and I are walking down to the pavilion," she said. "Maybe you should sit here and rest. We'll be back in a bit."

I was quiet. As they walked away I could feel my anger building. Certain situations bothered me to the point of feeling pressure in my chest, and this was one of them. I leaned back and looked to the sky, where a hawk soared in the clouds. For a while I lay there until I felt well enough to stand. Then I unzipped my pants and relieved myself freely in the wind, wavering my stream back and forth in the dirt the way I did when I was a little boy pissing in the yard. I zipped up and followed the trail back to the car to wait for them. Then I climbed up on the hood of the car. I lay back with my hands behind my head, staring into the sky. Clouds overhead were moving. I felt the sting of blood on my forehead, and when I touched it the pain only made me hate Nora worse. I spent ten minutes thinking of ways to hurt her. I made a decision to never forget that day, to never forget dumb Nora Drake, who later died on January 19, 2003 of strangulation.

Rosemary felt guilty about the way Nora had treated me, so she invited me to a movie the next Saturday afternoon in the old theatre downtown. One thing that always interested me about old theatres, I told her on the drive there, was how they felt so decayed and haunted, especially when only a few people were in the audience. As it turned out, we happened to see a slasher film, one of the *Nightmare on Elm Street* films, which Rosemary found particularly in sync with everything she loved about movies. "I need to be freaked out," she said, referring to the movies, otherwise why go?

"Maybe to laugh or cry," I said.

"No."

"Maybe to see Tom Cruise."

"Fuck him. No."

"So to be freaked out."

"To be scared out of your mind."

The theatre itself was old and on the verge of closing down due to the construction of a newer five-screen cinema being built near the interstate, and the remaining employees who worked the ticket booth and concession stand were "drug heads," as Rosemary called them, who either didn't finish high school or had dropped out.

After the movie ended and the credits were rolling, she suggested we stay and wait for everyone to leave. The usher, a guy with a crew cut who wore a black and gold vest, walked down the aisle with a broom and dustpan. He walked all the way to the front and then back again, sweeping up candy wrappers and trash, walking by us but not acknowledging we were still there.

"That guy doesn't give a shit," she said.

"About what?" I asked.

She looked back and watched him turn to head back to the lobby, and suddenly we were alone in the theatre. "Come on," she said, and headed down the aisle.

I followed her, silent, not knowing where we were going. We walked to the front of the theatre and up the stairs on the side, near the emergency exit. There was a big, heavy red curtain, and Rosemary told me to follow her behind it. I did so, not even reluctantly, because by then she could've told me to do anything and I would've done it. She could've told me to attack the usher and stab him to death, I would've done it, not to impress her, but because she had some unknown power over me.

There was a black door behind the curtain that she opened, and I followed her into the room it led to, which was an area behind the theatre screen. It was pitch dark in there, but a light blinked on and I saw that Rosemary had turned it on, which was surprising since she knew exactly where the switch was.

"We used to come back here after the late movies," she said.

"Who?"

"We could do whatever we wanted. I've been coming back here for years."

I saw a red velvet rope, empty boxes scattered around the room, and old movie posters stacked against the wall. There was a broken projector on the floor, and more boxes full of stacks of paper. As I walked around the room I saw something move to my left and realized it was my reflection in a cracked mirror. I looked at myself and barely recognized what I saw, my hair in my face, my skin looking sickly and pale. The walls were black, and I found myself staring at the pipes that ran along the walls to the ceiling.

"We did it back here," Rosemary said. "That was a couple of years ago."

"Who?" I asked.

She unhooked the red velvet rope and sat cross-legged on the floor, behind the giant screen. She ran her hand up and down on the rope, squeezing it. I waited, silent, for whatever she was going to do next.

She looked up at me then. "So what should we do?" she asked. "Do you want to hear all the details about what we did back here? Come over here. It's sort of gruesome if you want the truth."

"Who?" I said again.

But she looked away and I saw that the usher with the crew cut was suddenly standing slouched at the door, still holding his broom and dustpan, watching us. How long had he been there? What did he hear? I wondered: were we in trouble?

"The manager says you have to leave or he's calling the police," the usher said.

"How does he know I'm here?" Rosemary asked him. "Did you happen to tell him? Is that what happened? Are you going to tell on us, friend?"

The usher looked at his watch, slightly embarrassed. He looked like he was out of it, completely high, based on his bloodshot eyes and overall awkward demeanor.

"He's serious this time," the usher mumbled.

"Whatever."

As we walked out she stared at him, very directly, as if she were trying to intimidate him with the look, which seemed to work, because the usher almost cowered as she walked by him. I knew then the influence she had over people, including me, was dangerous.

"We'll go back again sometime and do it," she told me on the drive home.

"Do what?" I asked, but she still didn't answer me, turning down Rockland Road too fast, swerving around roadkill.

SHE STARTED TELLING ME to do things like make her bed, or remove the sheets so that she could sleep on the floor, or take all the trash from the upstairs bathroom and put it in the basement trash only to annoy Harold, who never grew angry or irritated enough to say anything about it. I never said anything; I did whatever she asked.

One Saturday morning she put jars of peanut butter and loaves of bread into a paper sack and informed me we were going downtown to a parking lot where she knew some homeless people. The homeless shelter was overcrowded after the economy had tanked and some people were forced to fend for themselves and find shelter wherever they could until the cops ran them away. Sure enough, when we got there a man wearing a flowery dress and black army boots and carrying a red leather purse told us the camp had moved to a site near the river.

"You'll find it on the east side," he told us. "The cops raided last week, so everyone left."

"I'm looking for Eunice," Rosemary said. "Do you know her?"

"Eunice? Eunice who?"

"I don't know her last name. She's an older Indian woman from the Osage."

The guy was digging through his purse. "Sorry," he said.

We drove out of town, following a winding road that led through the trees and down to Black River. The area on the east side of the river was more secluded than the west side, with more trees and fewer campsites and picnic tables. From the car we could see the tents, the only ones in winter, so we knew it was the homeless community. When we parked, we saw a man poke his head out of his tent and look.

"They're afraid of another raid," Rosemary said, reaching over the seat for the paper sack. "I don't blame them. But I think the cops patrol out here more in summer than winter."

We got out of the car and she walked ahead of me. In the distance, past the river, I could see the bridge leading to the road with the pawn shops and welding supply stores, near the YWCA. On the other side of the tents, a few people were sitting on blankets and playing cards. The earth was hard and frozen, only dirt and dead grass. The area smelled of wet leaves and cigarette smoke. When people saw us they weren't afraid or worried, and I wondered if others brought them food and such.

A man named Charlie came over and asked if we were looking for anyone. He was skinny and wore an old jean jacket with a frayed collar.

"We're looking for Eunice," Rosemary said.

He pointed toward a tent a little way farther down the path. "She's in one of those tents down there," he said. He looked at the sack. "You bring food?"

"We brought peanut butter and bread," she said. She reached into the sack and gave him a loaf of bread and a jar of peanut butter. He looked surprised and thanked us repeatedly. Another man, older with a beard and wearing a rain jacket too big for him, came over and introduced himself as Carl. He said he knew Eunice's tent and led us down the path to where she was. We followed him until we reached a dark green tent, where Carl called for her. The tent pitched there was large enough to hold a small family. I smelled urine and looked around, and a moment later came the smell of marijuana, but I couldn't see anyone smoking. I would've liked to smoke a little. I looked at Rosemary, but she was trying to look inside Eunice's tent.

A moment later Eunice emerged, holding a small gray cat in her arms. She looked very happy to see Rosemary.

"We brought you some bread and peanut butter," Rosemary said.

Eunice put the cat down and took the sack from Rosemary. Eunice was a sleek, white-haired woman with dark skin and beads around her neck. She was short and looked too frail to be living out there in the cold.

"Oh, sweetheart, I have something for you, too," she said. "Give me just a minute." She went back inside the tent, and Rosemary leaned in and told me that Eunice was a tough old woman, that she had family on the reservation but chose to struggle out here to show her sacrifice and compassion for God.

"Everyone thinks she's crazy," she said. "She covered herself in the woods with a blanket of leaves. She slept in the brush and fasted for thirty days. That's when she saw the spirits. They were like ghostly figures that came to her. They told her to sacrifice everything."

I looked at the tent. There was a garbage bag beside it, and past it, farther along the path, I could see a man dragging an inflatable mattress out of a tent. A moment later Eunice came out of the tent with beads and handed them to Rosemary. She put them around her neck.

"Beautiful," Eunice said.

Carl waved me over and invited me to sit with him. He was happy when I offered him a cigarette. We sat in plastic folding chairs beside a tree and smoked. He told me about working on the railroad back in the sixties and seventies before it went under in 1980. For a while he worked maintenance at the high school until budget cuts forced him out. He gambled away all his retirement on horse races and found himself moving north to stay with friends.

"It got worse and worse," he said. "My wife Darlene worked at the fried onion burger joint and then she left me," he said. "I try to tell myself I have my health, but I'm worried about that."

I turned and looked at Rosemary, who was talking very seriously to Eunice about something. Eunice placed her hand on Rosemary's shoulder and patted it gently.

A man with long hair shambled toward us and sat in another folding chair. He wore a blue coat and work boots. In his hand he had a pack of cigarettes and offered me one. I showed him my own pack and then lit his cigarette for him.

"I'm Jessie," he said.

"I'm Sequoyah."

He looked at Carl. "Any word from Sideshow?"

"Nothing." Carl looked at me. "Sideshow's a guy who was here with us," he said. "He was eighty-sixed last week and we haven't seen him since."

"He spent a few days in detox," Jessie said. "A few months ago he was selling himself for prescription codeine and benzos. He needs to come back."

We could hear the roar of a train blaring through in the distance.

"How long do you plan on staying here?" I asked them.

"Until I can get back on my feet," Carl said. "Hopefully the cops will leave us alone. It's our goddamn fundamental right to be left alone."

I counted twelve tents. The groups of people huddled around the fire, the garbage sacks piled beside tents, the woman sitting alone talking to herself, the bicycles turned over on their sides, the old mattresses and sleeping bags and rushing river—it was all so hard for me to comprehend people living this way. Their freedom was a freedom I couldn't understand or appreciate despite my upbringing, despite my short time in youth shelters, foster homes, and time alone when my mother was out at night. These people were making a decision to live this way. What I liked most about them was how they never stared at my face, or asked me what had happened. It was as if they saw right through me.

Rosemary and I left. As we pulled away I could see Carl and Jessie looking out over the river, and Eunice walking back to her tent with her cat. "This was a good idea," I said.

"I'm glad you came," Rosemary said.

I was happy to spend all this time with only Rosemary. Doing so helped me draw closer to her, and hopefully helped her see me as an important part of her life. We went for a soda at the Sonic Drive-In, just the two of us. Then we went for coffee at the diner downtown.

One day she drove me to the home of Ruth Arviso, a woman who'd helped raise her when she was little. Ruth was like a grandmother to her, she told me. They took walks together in the mornings and picked blackberries. Ruth Arviso taught her how to sew. They often went to a park and played. Ruth Arviso, she said, was the only woman who held her when she was little and told her how smart she was. Rosemary said she needed me to go along because Ruth was in poor health and suffering from Alzheimer's, barely able to talk, and now in home care and living with her daughter, a woman Rosemary said made her so livid she was afraid she would hurt her unless someone was there to calm her. And so I rode along as she drove to Ruth Arviso's house. She lived on the outskirts of town, and late in the afternoon we drove north, past open fields sprawling in the distance. I saw geese flying low over a pond. Low clouds hung in the sky. We finally turned down a long stretch of road leading to her house.

"She won't recognize me," Rosemary told me before we got out of the car. "She's sick with Alzheimer's, so she won't recognize me. She won't know anything. I just want you to know."

"All right," I said.

We got out of the car and walked to the front porch, and Rosemary knocked on the screen door. A moment later a woman appeared. She was petite, wearing a headscarf and dressed in a sweatshirt and blue jeans. She looked exhausted and didn't appear to register who Rosemary was until she said her name, then the woman opened the door without saying anything.

We entered the house, which was warm with a furnace on as well as a fire going in the fireplace. Ruth Arviso was sitting in a recliner with a blanket over her. I thought she must've been cold natured because it was exceedingly warm in the house, but then I saw how thin and fragile she looked as we sat across from her on the couch. There was a small TV across the room with poor reception, some old movie was on. The walls were pale and covered with framed photographs of family members. There was also a large cross hanging above the fireplace, so I gathered they were religious. The woman who let us in asked if we wanted coffee or tea, which Rosemary wanted but I didn't, and while she was in the kitchen Rosemary told me the woman's name was Geraldine, Ruth's daughter, and she was very rude and mean-spirited.

"Watch out for her," she whispered, then looked at Ruth and said hello.

Ruth looked at her, then me, then back at Rosemary. Her face was pale and drawn, and I could tell she was confused.

"Someone went to fetch your brother," she said.

Rosemary sat forward, and I could see the hurt on her face. Ruth touched her hair, patting it down. Her hands were fidgety, she sat with them in her lap, rubbing her knuckles like she had arthritis. From the light of the lamp beside her, I could see her hands were freckled, all bone. She wore no rings.

"It's Rosemary," Rosemary said. "How are you feeling?"

"I need my medicine," she said, looking around. "Where is Betsy?"

A moment later Geraldine returned from the kitchen with a glass of iced tea for Rosemary. She sat in the rocking chair beside Ruth and crossed her legs.

"What brings you out here?" she asked.

"We were driving around and I thought of Ruth," Rosemary said. "So we decided to stop by and see her. This is Sequoyah."

Geraldine gave me a look that was a forced smile, but she didn't say anything to me, so I kept quiet.

"How's she doing?" Rosemary asked.

"About the same," she said. "Wait a minute. When was the last time you were here?"

"Last summer."

"Right," she said. "It's progressed."

"The Alzheimer's?"

"Yes."

Ruth was now going through the papers on the table beside her. There was a newspaper, some other papers. She shuffled through them.

Out of nowhere I felt a strong desire to laugh. The thought of it mortified me, laughing at such a serious, sad time. I put my head down and stared at the shag carpet. Rosemary and Geraldine kept talking, about people they both knew, about Ruth's health, the Alzheimer's, and constant nurse care. The whole time they talked I found myself staring at the floor, frightened at the thought of laughing. Geraldine must've thought I was strange.

Then Rosemary went over to Ruth and took her hands, but Ruth withdrew them and looked up at her, horrified.

"I just wanted to stop by and say hi," Rosemary said. "Are you feeling okay?"

I saw Ruth's jaw trembling.

"We're going now, but I hope you take care," Rosemary said. She leaned forward to try to hug her, but Ruth seemed to pull away. Rosemary's back was to me, so I couldn't see her face.

Geraldine walked us to the door. "We expect she'll get worse," she said. "That's what they're telling us. The next step is the nursing home."

"I don't know what to say," Rosemary said.

"There's nothing to say."

"I'm so sorry. I have such good memories. It's so hard to think about."

"Take care," Geraldine said.

I heard the door close as we walked to the car. We got in and Rosemary lit a cigarette. She backed out of the drive and we headed south in the last light of the day. I stared out the window at the trees and old wood-framed houses, and Rosemary cried the whole drive home.

THAT NIGHT IN BED, in the dark, George was having trouble sleeping and kept me awake. He talked about wanting to buy a necklace. He thought he would look good in a necklace with his shirt off. "Our Osage neighbors, the Kagachees, make bead necklaces and bracelets," he told me. "They make them from rocks and the sticky substance found in porcupine quills. I bet they would make me one."

I sat up in bed and looked over at him. He was lying on his back, talking to the ceiling.

"Mr. Kagachee is so cool," he said. "He cuts the skins of rattlesnakes with a boning knife. He makes belts and hatbands. I want to be like him. He wears ceremonial feathers in his hair and chants traditional Indian songs. You should meet him. I mean you should meet them since you're an Indian too."

The remark felt racist, but I refrained from telling him.

He went on to talk about a festival in town with live music, food, and T-shirts designed and sold by the Kagachee family.

"Go to sleep," I told him.

"The Raider Halfway House out on Mulligan Road hosts karaoke. There's a pancake breakfast at the Methodist church sometimes."

"Go to sleep, George."

Five minutes later he finally did.

In the middle of the night, Rosemary woke me, placing a finger to her lips, and I followed her downstairs to the dark basement, where Harold always worked. She turned on the light and walked over to his desk, opening a drawer. I stood watching her, still half asleep, unsure of the time or what I was even doing.

"Jackpot," she said, and held up a baggie of marijuana.

I was still squinting from the brightness of the room. "Is that Harold's?" I asked. "Harold gets high?"

"Yep."

"Why did you wake me?"

"Why do you think?" She sprinkled the weed into a rolling paper.

"What time is it?" I asked.

"Almost three."

She stopped and looked at me, full of pity or disappointment. "When is a better time to smoke than the present? You can sleep in tomorrow."

I sat across from her, and she told me she fell asleep easier when she was high. She lit the joint and handed it to me. We shared the joint, passing it back and forth, neither of us speaking. Quickly I felt high and waved the rest of it away.

We talked for a while, about nothing serious or important. She told me about a dream in which her teeth fell out. She told me about waking up some nights in a panic without understanding why. The thought of dying in a car accident excited her, being thrown through a windshield. She was more afraid of living than dying.

I started looking through Harold's desk drawers, flipping through papers, looking for something, anything. I don't know what I was searching for. I saw numbers and figures written everywhere in pencil. I saw lists of names and phone numbers. I saw dollar amounts next to some names, check marks next to others. There were pro football teams and college teams with numbers next to them. Patriots minus six and a half. Raiders plus three. Bulls minus ten. The writings of a bookie, everything documented in notebooks. Records over the past few years. There were lists of names for several pages.

In another drawer he kept nasal spray, a bottle of aspirin. In another I found a can of foot powder. In another a pornographic magazine of older women. I flipped through it but found myself bored by it. "These women," I said.

"Yeah, they're gross," Rosemary said.

"All the makeup. The guys are disgusting."

"It's all so gross. Put it away."

Soon we were bored and went back upstairs, still high. "I'm going to bed," Rosemary said. "What are you going to do? Are you coming?"

"I don't know. Maybe a snack."

She waved me off and went upstairs. I went into the kitchen, where I found part of a peanut butter and jelly sandwich on a plate that George hadn't finished earlier. The room was blue from the moonlight in the window. I held my hand up and looked at it. The walls, the cabinets, everything was blue. I picked up the sandwich and peeled the bread apart. Then I took a knife from the drawer and sat cross-legged on the kitchen floor, stabbing the bread into shreds before devouring it.

At school, a few students told me they were in love with Rosemary: there was Farah LeClaire, who was pale and wore black lipstick and who evidently practiced witchcraft in the middle of the night with a group of girls from nearby Broken Arrow.

There was Valerie Day, a senior who worked part-time at the Whittington School for the Blind and had been suspended, twice, for masturbating in class.

And then there was a boy named Jerry Hock, who told me he had developed an anomalous obsession with Rosemary and had been watching her for months. Jerry was sixteen and washed dishes at a diner that served fried-onion hamburgers, and he suffered from heart tremors and told me he had only a year, maybe eighteen months to live, and that the one girl he planned on marrying in heaven was Rosemary.

"She's the real thing," he told me in the school hall. "I hope she hasn't fucked a lot of folks." Jerry played bass guitar in a gospel band every Sunday at a small nondenominational country church located in an old warehouse near the highway. He was thin and tall and slightly bucktoothed.

He had an annoying habit of sucking his teeth sometimes when he talked.

Jerry said he had a stack of books on Indian tribes I could have and invited me over to his house, so after school George and I rode bikes all the way over there, past the Shell station and Jimmy's Auto Parts, past the coffee shop where old men always sat inside drinking coffee and smoking cigarettes, over the railroad tracks and down Union Street to Jerry's house at the end of the block. Mr. Hock, Jerry's dad, invited us in and sat across from us in the living room. He told us we could call him by his first name, Jim, if that would make us comfortable. Mr. Hock wore thick-lensed glasses and a burgundy cardigan and spoke in a gentle voice.

"Would you boys like tea or milk or anything?" he said. "We have snacks. You must be thirsty."

A young girl peeked her head around the corner of the recliner where Mr. Hock sat. The girl was holding a Barbie doll and seemed to be studying us. She wasn't smiling. We declined the drinks and asked if Jerry was in his room.

"He is in his room," Mr. Hock said. "Are you sure you're not thirsty? We have juice or milk. I think we have orange juice."

The girl made a mean face and hid behind the recliner. Mr. Hock stood and fingered one of the buttons on his cardigan. "You're both perspiring," he said. "I should turn the heat down." The girl behind the recliner was hitting something against the floor. Mr. Hock inhaled deeply through his nose as if thinking very seriously about something.

"Jerry's room is downstairs," he said.

We followed him through the kitchen and downstairs to the basement, where Jerry apparently slept and spent most of his time. Mr. Hock went back upstairs and left us in the dim room. There were no windows down there. In the corner of the room was Jerry's bed, which was unmade and had clothes piled on it. On a nightstand next to the bed there was an alarm clock, a roll of paper towels, and a spiral notebook. Clothes were scattered on the floor. A bass guitar was leaning against the wall next to an old amplifier with lots of knobs. Yearbook photos of Rosemary were pinned up on the walls. Jerry didn't seem surprised to see us. He showed us a pile of comics and sat on his bed and played his bass while George looked through them.

"Take any you want," he said. He sucked his teeth. "I'm not a collector. I just like to draw."

"What about the tribe books?" I asked.

"Sorry, I don't know what happened to them," he said. "My dad must've donated them or something since nobody ever read them. No offense."

He put his bass down and opened a drawer full of notebooks and colored pencils. He opened a large notebook of plain white paper and showed us a number of cartoon characters he'd drawn in pencil: Sylvester the Cat staring up at Tweety Bird in a birdcage; Yosemite Sam pointing a pistol at Bugs Bunny; the Road Runner tied to a railroad track and holding up a sign that says "Help!" as Wile E. Coyote, a napkin tied around his neck, stands over him with a fork and knife.

And then there were the more disturbing drawings, the ones of naked women and animals. There were several drawings of a girl with long hair in submissive poses. One showed her on her knees with her wrists tied behind her back. I wondered whether it was supposed to be Rosemary. George went back to the comic books and grabbed a few to take. Somehow, eventually, we were on our way back upstairs, out of the filthy and windowless den. Mr. Hock walked us to the door and held it open for us.

"You boys come back," he said.

Poor strange Jerry Hock. I was secretly fond of him. I expect we could be friends after all these years if I only knew where he lived.

AS THE DAYS PASSED I continued to have headaches and feel nauseated. Agnes took me to the doctor, where I was given a blood test and was diagnosed with a small ulcer. The doctor prescribed pills and I had to change my diet to less caffeine, no spicy foods, and no smoking.

I was told to relax more and keep myself busy: cleaning, organizing, drawing sketches. On a sick day home from school, I cleaned the upstairs bathroom, wiping down the sink and tub and shower, scrubbing the toilet, and spraying the mirror with Windex. I put the dirty towels in the hamper in the hallway, then folded the T-shirts in my dresser. I folded George's T-shirts, too.

Agnes stayed downstairs, leaving me alone. I spent the whole afternoon drawing at the desk while it rained outside. I decided to draw various things for Rosemary to show her I, too, had an interest in art, like she did. I wanted her to see I possessed a desire to paint and maybe even win an award like she had. I considered myself an average artist—I'd done well in junior high art, particularly with cartoons, and I had even won honorable mention in a contest at the school one year when I'd drawn a cartoon wolf with bandages on his nose and a patch over one eye. The inscription underneath it read: "Do What's Right! Don't Fight!"

I drew landscapes, objects of my desire, things to represent my longing for companionship in my time of sickness. This is how I remember it. I drew buildings on fire. I drew a clown holding a machine gun, and a dog frothing at the mouth. I drew an old man dead in a rocking chair. His head was slumped over and he was bleeding from his chest.

This went on all afternoon, during the rain and after it stopped, until George returned home from school. In the end, looking over them all, I elected not to give them to Rosemary, and instead ripped them all to shreds, ripping and ripping, tearing them into tiny pieces.

I took my pills and bore the stomach pain. I had also contracted some sort of slight head cold, I remember, because I was running a fever and had a sore throat. Those few days I missed school were mostly spent in boredom. I lay in bed all day, and when I wasn't sleeping I was lying there feeling drowsy and sensitive to noise. When I opened my eyes I longed to hear the sounds of birds outside, or Agnes moving around downstairs, sounds that helped me feel at peace and unafraid.

Most importantly, I recall being at Rosemary's beck and call, willing to do anything for her. I drifted in and out of fever dreams. I thought of warm summer afternoons, walking through a garden or sitting in the sun. And I dreamed of yellow leaves covering the bedroom, flying in through an open window. In the dream I got up and walked downstairs and found the whole house covered in yellow leaves. The windows downstairs were open and a flock of birds flew in, perching on the fireplace mantle and the backs of chairs and on shelves. The whole house was covered in yellow leaves and birds. I woke feeling hot and feverish. I was drowsy and weak and went downstairs for water and aspirin. Agnes made me chicken noodle soup. I went back upstairs and slept.

One late night Rosemary came to the doorway of my room and waved for me to follow her. George was asleep, so I got out of bed quietly and went into the hall. I followed her into her room and she closed the door.

"Agnes told me about your stomach problems," she said. "Sorry you're sick."

"I'm feeling better," I said.

She offered me a cigarette, which I accepted despite doctor's orders. We smoked and I stared at her through the pale smoke.

"I wanted to share a secret with you," she said. "I was in

juvenile detention a few years ago. It wasn't a big deal, I spent a weekend there and on Monday the judge released me to my caseworker."

I remembered what I'd read in her journal about being locked up. I pretended to act surprised by it.

"Really? What did you do?"

"We stole clothes from the mall. My friend Farah and I. They arrested us in front of everyone. It's a secret."

"Farah."

"Yeah, Farah. Do you know her?"

"No," I lied. "I think I know who she is. She's tough? Gets suspended?"

"Yeah, pretty much, but I don't talk to her anymore. She's supposed to stay away from me. Long story I won't tell. Anyway, in the detention center they restrained me. Then they put me on my stomach, facedown, when I began crying and yelling at them to stop because it hurt. Restraints aren't supposed to be painful unless you resist with a great struggle. I apparently did. They took my arms behind my back and put the leather restraints on my wrists, which put pressure on my head against the cement. The floor was cold and hard against my cheek. I must've been in shock or panic because I suddenly felt nothing, I remember not feeling anything, like everything around me disappeared. It sounds weird, but it was like I'd become in some strange way actually *attached* to the floor."

I leaned forward a little. "They did that? It hurt?"

"Yeah, it hurt," she said. "I heard a rushing sound of wind in my ears like the roar you hear when your head is completely out the window of a car on the highway, and this massive roar didn't go away until the pain from my arms went away, even though I continued to kick and yell and gag while they put the restraints on my ankles. I mean, even the kicking didn't do any good. I mean somebody must've been sitting on my legs, because I felt weight there and also on my back. Then I felt a hand near my mouth, so I bit someone's hand. Then I felt pressure on my whole body and heard the voices all around me saying, *Settle down!* and if I struggled to move I wasn't aware of it until I managed to close my eyes. I gave up finally. It was terrible. It was one of the worst things I've ever been through."

"Why did they restrain you?"

"I threatened suicide," she said. "They have to give girls razors if they ask for them in the shower so they can shave their legs. I broke down and told one of the officers I was going to start cutting my wrist with it. After they let me out I had a delinquent offense, but it was erased after I did community service."

"Oh shit," I said.

"So that's my secret. Now you tell me one."

The only secret I knew was that Harold kept a lot of money hidden in the shed, which I told her about. "George found it," I said. "He's known about it for a while and showed it to me. It's obviously a hiding place."

"I already knew about it," she said. "He keeps hundred dollar bills in stacks. I don't know why he's hiding it in the shed."

"I've never seen so much money."

"Sometimes people who live in the country bury money," she said. "They bury money for themselves. It's Harold's money, you know, since he's a bookie."

"We didn't take anything."

After only a few drags, I ground out my cigarette in the ashtray. It was the first cigarette I'd had in several days and it was making me light-headed. Rosemary set the ashtray on the window ledge and opened the window a little more. We heard the dog howling from outside again.

"I hate that fucking dog," she said. "He's sick. All he does is bark every goddamn night."

I stood and tried to look out, but there was only darkness. "I bet he's hungry. That's why he's howling. It sounds like he's crying."

"Dogs bark for no reason. They bark for attention. They bark because they hear shit twenty miles away."

"Maybe he's hungry," I said.

"I want you to do something for me," she said. "Get rid of that dog for me, okay?"

"What do you mean?"

"Shoot him," she said. "Kill him, whatever. Or just scare him away. Would you do that for me?"

I looked out the window.

She got up and opened her closet door and told me to come have a look. Inside the closet I saw a rifle.

"Is it a BB gun?" I asked.

"Sort of."

"What does that mean?"

"It's a .22, which is a little bit heavier. I've had it for a couple of years. I took it from a friend. It's light, only like three pounds."

I went to the bed and sat down.

Her mouth curved at the corners. She studied me. "It's an animal, not a person. Would you do it for me?"

"I'll do it if you want," I said.

She handed me the rifle. It wasn't as heavy as it looked. Then we went downstairs quietly so we wouldn't wake anyone. We slipped out the back door and went out into the night. It was freezing and I could see my breath in front of me as we walked. We walked through the yard, past the shed. A little farther I could see it: a large dog, digging in the dirt. As we approached, it looked up at us.

"That dog has rabies," Rosemary said, motioning for me to stay back. "Look at him, Sequoyah."

I moved closer and quickly kicked the dog. It cowered and moved away, but then it turned and looked at us.

"He's not foaming at the mouth," I said.

"I saw him foaming," she said. "I saw it!"

The dog started digging into the dirt again.

"Shoot him!" Rosemary shouted. "Shoot him before he ruins everything. Before he gets aggressive!"

I moved closer and kicked the dog again, this time so hard the dog let out a whimper and started to run away. Then I aimed and fired. The gun went off and my eyes must've been closed, because I don't know where I shot. The dog ran off into the woods.

"You fucking missed," she said.

"He ran off," I said.

"You missed. It doesn't matter. Next time I'll shoot him myself."

This is how it was. She could've talked me into doing anything. She had talked me into killing a stray dog.

Later that night I lay wide awake in bed, thinking about the dog. And how ruthless she seemed about it, how much she hated it. I started hating it, too. I remember lying in bed thinking about it over and over, imagining myself holding that rifle, blasting some terrified animal into another life.

ROSEMARY LATER ASKED ME: "Do you ever think about dying?"

"I think about other people dying," I said.

"If you could choose how you had to die, what way would you choose? I would die in a fire. Or drowning. Or suffocation or being choked to death."

"Choking sounds good," I said.

"I'll just say there's something weird and wonderful about dying," she said. "There's something that moves me, deep inside. It's too hard to explain or to understand without actually experiencing it, unless we're there. I think of it as a circle we step inside. We feel something we can't feel right now, alive. Maybe inside the circle is a warmth that stimulates you and makes you feel weightless, floating on air without any effort, and there's a light of brightness inside you like no other light out there you've ever seen or felt. Does that make sense? The light is unidentifiable unless you experience it. A secret among secrets, a thing of movement. It's transcendence."

I stared at her bottom lip, which was red with lipstick. It was dark, the color of dried blood. I wanted to have her mouth for my own. I liked her voice, especially when she talked quietly like this.

"I would die quick in my sleep," I told her.

"That's painless," she said.

No matter what, I could not bring myself to think of Rosemary any less. Little by little, the days were like thieves, stealing parts of me, including any courage I had to confront my feelings toward people: my growing interest in Rosemary, my hatred for Nora Drake, my friendship with George. At night I began to think more and more about my mother, as her court hearing grew closer. I worried about her release. I worried about her remaining locked up. And I worried the days were taking my feelings, how the more I thought about everyone, the more dead I felt inside.

Slowly, my body began to feel better physically. Around this time George and I started playing a game in which one of us was an intruder the other had to kill by pointing a water gun and shooting. It was a form of hide-and-seek but with a simulation of death attached. I don't remember whose idea it was to start playing, or why we started playing, only that we played for about a week or two. We took the game seriously, exaggerating death. We hid behind doors, crouched in dark hallways. The water guns shot a thin stream that reached almost across a room. You only needed one shot. George killed me upstairs in the tub, where I slumped to my death. He killed me by the stairs. He killed me outside by the elm. My deaths were dramatic, spent clutching my stomach and falling to my knees before collapsing. I shot him in the head one morning when he woke. I shot him in our closet. I found him under my bed and shot him there. I crept up behind him in the kitchen and shot him in the back. George's deaths were slow-motion, way more exaggerated than my own. He sidestepped after being shot, clutched his head or gut, held onto cabinets or tables to brace his fall, slowly, slowly dying until he reached out, always, before letting out one last breath.

To die, when the game ended at least for the time being, meant I needed to play harder, to take it more seriously, to be better.

To kill meant victory, a sense of accomplishment since it was never easy to find the intruder. To seek out, to find. To hunt and be hunted. It was a game of survival. A game of strategy and defense. The last time we played it, I pulled back the shower curtain and found George crouched down and begging for his life. I lifted him by the collar and pointed the water gun to his head. He closed his eyes and pleaded for me to let him live.

"Intruder!" I yelled, and shot him dead.

After that, George quit playing. His reason was he was bored with dying, he said. Dying and killing each other had exhausted itself, unfortunately, though I was sad to stop playing.

I wanted to hunt and be hunted. Growing up without a sibling, and even at the shelter or in foster homes, I had never played anything like it before. At school, some of the guys in my grade played Dungeons & Dragons, a fantasy role-playing game, and soon everyone was talking about their characters at school as if they were real people. We wanted to exist in other worlds. We wanted to lose our own sense of reality, to be other people with other lives. Lives unlike anyone else's.

"It's fun to hunt the intruder," I told George.

"I'm tired of hiding, Sequoyah. You always find me. The house doesn't have any new hiding places. We've used them all."

He was right. We used the same hiding places all over the house, which made the hunt less challenging. Still, I found myself longing for the thrill of sneaking up on him and catching him when he wasn't expecting it. I liked moving quietly throughout the house, seeking him out. We had started hiding outside, but even that grew boring at some point.

One afternoon Harold came into the bedroom and asked whether we had seen Rosemary. I hadn't seen her but assumed she was at work. George confirmed her work schedule.

"That's funny," Harold said. "I thought she said she was off today. What do you make of that?"

George and I were both quiet. It was rare to see Harold upstairs unless he was in his bedroom with the door closed, and it was even rarer to see him standing in the doorway of our bedroom. From the angle where I was sitting on my bed, he somehow looked taller.

Harold asked us, "Have you guys been outside today by chance? In the shed?"

We told him we hadn't, at which point George asked why he was asking.

"No reason," he said. He was looking at the floor, thinking. "I was looking for something but it'll turn up."

He turned and left. George went back to writing in his notebook without saying anything about it, so I spoke.

"What do you think that meant?" I asked. "What was he talking about?"

"I don't know."

"You think he knows we found his money?"

"Money?" George said, and tapped his pen against his chin. "Oh, I don't think so. I bet he's just looking for something. He misplaces things all the time. He's so secretive, he probably hides his own shoes."

A little while later Harold was back in our doorway again, this time asking us for help. "I need to go up to the attic," he said. "You guys mind helping me out?"

We agreed and followed him into the hallway, where he reached up and pulled the cord that lowered the stairs leading to the attic. We climbed the stairs and Harold turned on the light. We found ourselves in a dusty attic filled with boxes. It smelled of cedar and mothballs.

The room was full of boxes of useless items: batteries,

steel-wool buffer pads, poker magazines, paperback books, and comic books. There were kerosene lamps and cloth-covered picture albums. There were flashlights and paintbrushes and spiral notebooks and old greeting cards. There were boxes of toys: wind-up plastic boats, racecars, a wooden Mickey Mouse doll, a stuffed teddy bear, a miniature birdcage, a tiny plastic house with a red roof, and so on.

"There are so many things in here I don't know what's trash and what isn't," Harold said. "Once a year I come up here to bring down the Christmas decorations, all these boxes full of ornaments." He tapped his toe on a box, and I saw Christmas ornaments sprinkled with glitter, holly berries, strands of silver tinsel, and tangled strings of blinking lights. I ran my hand along the curved back of a wicker chair while George blew the dust from an old cigar box. When he opened it there was nothing inside.

"I'm building a bookshelf for our bedroom," Harold said. "Somewhere there are shelves in here, but I forgot where I put them. Look around."

"Are you sure you didn't put them in the shed?" George asked.

"I already looked there," he said. "I think they're in here somewhere."

We couldn't find them. We looked everywhere and they weren't there. Harold seemed confused.

"I guess I just don't get it," he said. "They're definitely not in here."

We climbed back down and followed him into his bedroom. Harold reached into his dresser for a pencil and placed it behind his ear. He turned to us. "What we need to do," he said, "is pull the bed away from the wall for a minute. The frame's got wheels."

The bed was huge: a king-size with a burgundy comforter and four large pillows. George and I pushed the headboard while Harold, kneeling, pulled from the other end. We slid it a few feet away from the wall. He came over and examined the wall. "The shelves will go here," he said, "all six of them."

"Are you putting them up today?" I asked.

He shook his head. "I need to figure out where those shelves are first. I bought them a couple of years ago. It's a lot of work. There's measuring. There's sanding and polishing. I need a new hobby. I'm a sports buff. Too many games on and I need to keep my mind occupied. It's not easy." He produced a tape measure that was clipped to his belt loop and had George hold one end of the tape measure against the floor while he stretched it vertically, then horizontally, drawing two little marks on the wall with the pencil. "Right," he said. "Okay, that's good. Let's push the bed back where it was."

George and I pushed it back.

"Thank you, boys," he said. "I guess that's all we can do for now. Oh, by the way, have you guys been out to the shed lately?"

George looked at me.

"Not really," I said. "Why?"

He looked at his watch. "Never mind. Something's missing. I need to make a phone call downstairs."

We followed him out of the room and he went downstairs. George and I stood in the hallway, watching him. When he got to the bottom of the stairs he stopped for a moment and looked at his watch, then walked away.

"I think he knows we found his money in the shed," George said.

"That's what I told you," I said.

He cocked his head, thinking. "You didn't say anything to Rosemary, did you?"

"No."

"Are you sure?"

"I'm positive."

"Well, I'm going to meditate," he said.

"Meditate?" I said. "When did you start meditating?"

"Since last year. I read an article by a swami called 'Meditation on the Self and Super Conscious.' It talks about three different stages in meditation. Do you want to read it?"

"No."

"Well, if you do it's on my bookshelf. I'll just need some quiet time alone, if you don't mind."

"I said I don't want to read it," I told him.

George bowed his head in gratitude and headed down the hall to our room. I went downstairs to the living room, where Agnes was dumping an ashtray full of cigarette butts and ashes into a wastebasket. She carried the wastebasket into the kitchen and returned with her purse over her shoulder. "I'm going to the grocery store," she said. "I'll be back later. Rosemary's at work but Harold's downstairs in his office if you need anything."

I watched her walk out the front door. Through the front window I saw her get into her car, back out of the drive and pull away. I was standing alone in the living room. Even though Harold was downstairs and George was upstairs, I felt as though I was the only one there.

I sat looking at photo albums for an hour. Photos of Harold and Agnes, their wedding, on vacation, playing golf. Photos of people I didn't know. Photos a decade old. People in bell-bottom pants and long hair. Photos of houses, children, pets. Photos of Rosemary and George.

One photo of Rosemary, asleep on the same couch where I was sitting, caught my attention. Something about her expression, mouth curled downward, made me think she wasn't really asleep. With her eyes closed, she looked angry or upset about something. It was such a strange and interesting photo that whoever snapped it must've known she was faking. She was lying on her side, eyes closed, part of her hair covering her face. And I, too, lay on my side, taking her same position, right there on the same couch. And I, too, closed my eyes and curled my mouth downward, attempting to replicate the expression as best as I could. I wanted someone to take my picture. Maybe someone would find me, I thought, and snap a photo the way they did of Rosemary. Years later we would look at it and laugh. Years later someone would ask all sorts of questions about me, and Harold would tell them I was a good boy with a good mind. I kept my eyes closed. I stayed in that position until my face began to hurt, then I opened my eyes to an empty room.

There was some dissent between Rosemary and Harold. I could sense it in the way she acted around him and fell quiet in his presence. And I could see the frustration in his face when he looked at her, though I didn't hear them argue. When she spoke to him, she wouldn't look at him. She crossed her arms, lowered her head so that her hair fell over and covered her face.

I began to study her more and more. She let me watch her sit in front of her mirror and put on makeup, put on jewelry, pick out her shoes. She let me watch her sit by the window and smoke in the moonlight, with the window cracked open and the sounds of the cold wind blowing outside. When she wasn't aware, I watched her walk from the dinner table to the kitchen, from the kitchen to the stairs, from the front door to her car in the driveway. I watched her grip the handrail of the staircase when she started upstairs. I watched her sit cross-legged in her room when she put on headphones and closed her eyes to the music. Her posture was better than mine or anyone else's. Her skin was tan and darkened near the elbows. I watched the way she sat on the floor, pulling her knees to her chest. I watched the way she sat cross-legged on the edge of the bed, and the way she tilted her head to listen, like she was really interested in whatever I was saying.

As much as I watched her, other times I would refuse to look at her. I refused to look at her as we sat across from each other at the dinner table. I refused to look at her in the car when she drove us to school. When she looked at me I looked away, avoiding eye contact, as if looking directly at her in the eyes would convey some great meaning. I wasn't able to understand what I was feeling. And yet I imagined her wearing my clothes, shirts and coats, as if it meant we shared some sort of connection. I imagined her sleeping in my favorite T-shirt, a royal blue Ocean Pacific brand shirt with a graphic of a surfer riding a wave and the orange sun setting behind him. I thought of her wrapping herself in my bedsheet or blanket, walking down the hall in the middle of the night to find me and let me know she needed to wear my clothes to keep my scent close to her, to breathe me in, to keep me near. That she needed to cut my hair, tie it with a rubber band and keep it in a bottle. To open the bottle was like opening perfume, filling the room with me.

And for her to tell me this would never sound strange or sad because I would feel the same. I would wrap myself in her bedsheet or blanket, wear her clothes, cut her hair and put it in a bottle to keep with me. When I needed to, I could open the bottle to smell her. I could fill the room with her presence, her scent, her spirit. By both of us doing this, we would share in a ritual, something we would never be able to define or understand. My hair was long, but hers hung down past her shoulders. I wanted to grow my hair longer to be like hers. In a strange way we could pretend to be each other, though I would never mention such a thing.

Then one night she looked at me silently and said she thought things couldn't get any worse.

"What do you mean?" I asked.

"I don't know."

"What is it?"

But she wouldn't tell me anything.

I went to the window and pressed my face against the glass. I couldn't see anything outside but darkness.

AS SHE BEGAN TO mention death more in our late night conversations, Rosemary confessed to me that she had written a letter to be read after she passed. She showed me only the first line, which read: "I aspire to the condition of the spirit."

"Read the whole thing," I said.

"That's all you get until I'm dead."

"No."

"There's more and more and more."

As days passed she retreated to her room and asked that

I not bother her. I found it hurtful—it was as if she was no longer interested in me, like she'd grown bored with my company. Had I not been talkative enough? Did she already understand me better than I even understood myself? Thoughts raced through my mind as to why she was slowly distancing herself, slowly becoming less involved in my life, less interested in anything.

When I asked her to get coffee, she declined. She didn't want to go to Sonic. I even suggested we take food back to the homeless camp at Black River, but she said she was too tired. "I'm just really, really tired lately," was her excuse. "I feel like my body is worn out."

"From what?" I asked.

"Everything."

I didn't want her retreating from me, losing interest. When I told George about it, he said it was normal behavior for her. He sat in our room, writing in his notebook. His tongue protruded slightly from his mouth as he brought the notebook closer to his face and squinted at it.

"You think she's depressed?" I asked.

"She's just quiet like that. She's moody. It's just her."

"She seems different."

George turned the page in his notebook, wrote something down and tore out the sheet. He brought it over and handed it to me. In capital letters, underlined twice: DON'T WORRY!

But I did worry. I'd saved some money from past jobs, mowing yards, cleaning out garages, loading a junk truck for a friend of my mother, and I was super thrifty, spending my earned money only on cigarettes, an emergency fund. I decided, on a whim, that I would buy a bunch of little gifts for her to cheer her up. After all, I told myself, it wasn't the price of the gift, but the thought that counts. So one Saturday morning, George and I went to a garage sale and I bought a bunch of stuff for ten dollars.

In my dresser I kept a list of everything I would give her in case I needed to remind her of the gifts I had given. I liked to keep an inventory of gifts or nice gestures I did for people to remind them in case they ever wronged me. I also kept a list of the people who'd hurt me throughout my life, mostly involving kids from previous schools who had made comments about my face, or about my clothes, or about anything that hurt my feelings. It didn't seem strange at the time to do such things.

I gave her a Disney princess pen with a pink feather attached to the eraser, and a greeting card with a photo of two white kittens on the front. Inside the card I wrote, "You have a face I want to have." I also gave her a clown figurine and an old doll. I put them into a sack and gave it to her.

She took them out of the sack, one by one, and placed them on her bed.

"Your face isn't bad," she said.

"Yours is better."

"Don't be ashamed of yours."

"When I was little I wanted to be someone else."

"When I was little I dreamed of magical lands," she said. "There were giant lollipops and marching bands with music that filled the air and brought kids running from all over. I drew pictures in crayon of angels and dogs. Those were my first drawings. The stories I liked to read all dealt with children escaping wolves or held prisoner."

We lay on the floor, listening to "Venus in Furs" by The Velvet Underground. For a while neither of us said anything. We listened to X. We listened to Robert Smith sing about dark things. I walked my fingers across her leg, up to her hip. I fluttered my hand like a bird.

She was reading something from her journal and showed it to me. "You want to know something personal about me?" she said, showing me the open book.

I sat up and read:

> *I was placed here for shoplifting and taking a bunch of pills. They have me on all this medication here which does nothing except make me sleepy. Dr. Smith-Treson said those are side-effects that will go away with time. I asked her—"How long will I be here?" But she couldn't give me a clear answer. Today I'm pretending to be invisible because this place is horrible.*

"Was it terrible?" I asked.

"Pretty much."

I didn't want to tell her I'd spent time in juvenile detention.

It wasn't something that felt important at the time. I pretended to act like I was intrigued by the thought of being locked up.

"Lately I've been following the news story of a kid somewhere in Kansas," I told her. "He walked into school and shot another student. That almost never happens."

"You want to walk into school and shoot someone?" she asked. She laughed a little, like it was funny to think about. This bothered me. I opened my eyes and stared up at the ceiling. Shadows stretched across the ceiling like ghosts.

"I think Harold knows I took some money from him," she said. "Last year he caught me and freaked out. Ever since, he goes around thinking I'm trying to steal from him all the time. I've only taken like twice in the past year."

"He doesn't trust you," I said.

"He's a bookie. He doesn't trust anyone."

What I soon understood about Rosemary was that she was adept at answering questions without giving direct answers.

"I don't feel complete unless I know death is going to happen soon," she said. "If that makes sense? I'm so pissed at Harold right now. It makes me think about the point of life. Maybe the world is ending and we're all being held accountable for our actions."

"I don't know," I said. "I mean, you're trustworthy."

"I know people think I'm crazy for saying this, but everything points too strongly in that direction. The world is ending. Nobody needs a long life."

"You think people believe that?" I said. "The world is ending? Shit, nobody knows."

"Nobody needs a long life," she said again.

"I'm more afraid of dying in a horrible car accident or something," I said. "Or finding out I have cancer. And whatever happens after death. Maybe there's something."

"There's nothing," she answered.

One Saturday, an unusually warm day for winter, Rosemary suggested we go for a bike ride to the country, far from the house, far away, she said, to a secret place that felt like another world. I was ecstatic with the idea, thinking maybe she was coming out of her isolation, wanting to spend more time with me. Even though I didn't have a bicycle, there were four in the garage that I could choose from. Rosemary chose a red one with a basket in front and placed an old blanket in it. As I stood trying to decide what bicycle to ride, she decided for me, pointing to the blue one.

"That one," she said.

I followed her as we walked the bicycles out of the garage. The blue one, too, had a basket in front, along with a dented handlebar with worn grips, but I didn't mind. I hadn't ridden a bicycle in a very long time. I loved the sudden plunge of pedaling down the driveway and onto Comanche Road with my jacket zipped up and the cool wind in my face. As I think back, I consider that bicycle ride as one the most invigorating experiences during my stay at the Troutts. For me it was about undiscovered territory, full of strangeness and wonder, riding down hills and plunging into unknown areas. We rode past tall weeds, dark puddles, past old shacks and through pebbles scattered along the road. I pedaled behind Rosemary, following her, and soon we stopped beside the road and she pointed to a low-hanging branch with a pink bandanna tied to it.

"That's how I know where to turn," she said.

"You tied it?"

"I climbed it and tied it to that branch last year. Nobody's even stolen it. I think people who drive by must think it's a memorial or something."

We started down the trail into the woods that looked as if it hadn't been traveled in years. I imagined wolf tracks under my tires, coyotes and bobcats slinking around at night. Trees crowded us on both sides as we rode into the deep woods, coasting along the trail.

"I hope we don't see any snakes," I shouted, following, but Rosemary didn't respond. Then we came to a fork in the trail where she turned left and followed a narrow path, and I trailed behind her, gripping the handlebar firmly with both fists as I pedaled over dirt and old leaves and twigs. We came upon a clearing near a small hill that sloped down to a creek full of water from fresh rain. I got off the bicycle and leaned it on the kickstand. Over by the edge of the slope, I looked down at the streaming water and all the rocks and brush around it.

"This is the best place," Rosemary said.

"It's dark and quiet," I said. "Do you come here a lot?"

"When I don't want to be found."

"But why today?"

"I want you to see it, too."

She took the blanket from the basket on her bicycle, unfolded it and spread it on the dirt. I watched her slip off her shoes and sit down, digging into her purse. I sat across from her and watched her. She retrieved a cigarette from her purse and lit it with a lighter.

"Hope there aren't any snakes out here," I said.

She inhaled and smiled, then handed it to me. I took a drag on it and handed it back.

"Lie on your back and look up," she said, and I did so. We stared up into the ashen sky and I watched the top of the trees move.

"What do you see?" I asked. "What am I supposed to see?"

"Everything looks like we're at the bottom of a pit and looking out of it," she said.

"I don't know."

"I mean it looks like the world is up there and we're down here, deep underground. Like we're buried alive and nobody knows we're down here."

"Weird," I said, and soon we were both laughing. We sat up and I stared at her mouth.

"We should go down to the creek," she said.

"Why?"

I kept staring at her mouth and she frowned. "Come on," she said, standing, and I stood and followed her. We edged our way down the slope to the creek where water streamed past. It was cooler down there, and more shaded from the outside world, and I could see why Rosemary liked the spot so much, since it felt so secluded from everything. What a fantastic hiding place, I thought.

Rosemary knelt down and put her hand in the water, and I did the same. The water was freezing cold, and dark, and I felt the mossy rocks underneath. I withdrew my hand and dried it with my shirt.

"I dare you to pee in it," she said.

"The water? No way."

"Do it. You're too scared?"

"Whatever."

"You don't want me to see it, huh?"

She laughed and stood, shaking her wet hand. She wiped her hand on her jeans and looked down at me. "You afraid of snakes?" she asked. "Are you scared a snake will leap out and bite your dick if you do it?"

"It's not that."

"You're scared of me," she said.

"No."

She started back up the slope toward our bicycles. I stayed there, watching her walk.

"Where are you going?" I called out.

"Home," she said, without looking back at me. "Are you coming or not?"

"Why?" I said, standing. "Wait, let's stay!"

"You're scared, Sequoyah."

"Wait," I said again, hurrying up the slope, trying not to slip and fall.

AFTER THE LONG RIDE back along the road, past the dark puddles and old barns, after I trailed behind her on the dented blue bicycle, we finally made it home, and she asked me a question that surprised me. In the garage, as we leaned our bikes against the kickstands, she asked me if I would ever spy on her.

"What do you mean?" I said.

"Would you watch me when I wasn't aware? Would you do that?"

I stood there, unsure what to say.

"You always stare at my mouth," she said. "So I'm just wondering if you like to watch me when I'm not looking."

"Do you want me to? You want me to spy on you?"

She hooked her hair behind her ear and started for the door inside. "You're kind of freaking me out," she said.

Later that same afternoon, Liz called to remind me that my mother's court hearing was on Thursday. She would drive to Little Crow to pick me up and take me. She told me to wear a nice pair of slacks and a collared shirt.

"What do you think will happen?" I asked her.

"I'm just not sure," she said. "But you'll get a chance to visit with her before the hearing in a supervised visitation."

"So does this mean I'll get to go home with her?"

"I hope so, Sequoyah," she said. "But I want you to understand these things aren't that easy. She could get probation or she could be rejected. I don't want you to be too hurt if she's rejected."

"I know," I said.

When we got off the phone I went upstairs to my room and saw that George was asleep. I picked up the book Rosemary had given me and started reading. Thinking about my mother's parole hearing made me nervous, and I needed to keep my mind occupied with something else. About ten minutes into reading, George made a sound in his sleep. When I looked over at him I saw he was biting his bottom lip and grunting. I set the book down and went over to him and touched his arm. "George," I said, but he stirred and bit his lip so hard that it started bleeding. This time I shook him harder to wake him. "George," I said loudly. "Wake up, you're bleeding. George!"

He opened his eyes then blinked and stared at me, confused for a moment. Then he touched his lip and looked at the blood on his finger.

"You're bleeding," I said.

He looked at me again. Then he got out of bed and rushed out of the room. I heard him close the door to the hallway bathroom. I went back to my bed and started reading again.

A few minutes later he was standing in the doorway, holding toilet paper to his mouth. "What did you do?" he asked.

I smiled at him. "What?"

"What did you do to me?" he said again, this time louder.

I set the book down on the bed next to me. "I woke you up, George. You were having a bad dream or something. You were biting your lip so hard it started bleeding."

"I don't believe you," he said.

I laughed, turned away. I'm not sure why I was laughing at him. When I turned back, he looked confused, even afraid. It was the first time I'd seen him look at me in this way. Then he left, and I heard him walk down the hall and down the stairs.

Later that night I retreated to the attic to be alone. I climbed the stairs and sat, listening to music on my headphones. There was a dusty antique lamp on the floor next to where I sat. The longer I spent in there, the more I appreciated the room's smallness, its safety. Soon I saw a shadow emerging from the stairs. I expected to see George, and I secretly hoped for Rosemary, but when I looked up I saw Harold. In the shadows, he loomed in the doorway. He was smoking a cigarette, and in the dim light I could see the smoke trailing from it.

I turned off the Walkman and removed my headphones.

"Hey," he said. "Can I come in?"

"Sure," I said.

His footsteps were heavy on the wood floor. He found an old lawn chair, unfolded it, and brought it over to me and sat down. I pulled my knees to my chest and looked up at him. He was tall, and his legs looked abnormally long as he sat in front of me in the lawn chair while I sat on the floor, staring up at him.

"You doing okay?" he asked. He took a drag of his cigarette. I saw smoke settling around his face.

I nodded.

"Yeah? Good. Agnes was worried about you. She went into our bedroom and saw the stairs and knew you were up here. She thought maybe something was wrong."

"Nothing's wrong."

"That's good," he said. "I do the same thing in the basement. A man needs his time to himself." He reached for an empty soda can and ground his cigarette out on it. "One other thing," he said. "There's something else I want to ask you about."

I couldn't tell whether or not he was angry. I tried as quickly as I could to think of everything I might've done in the past day or two that might've offended him.

"There's some money missing," he said. "Some cash I keep in a private place. It isn't very much, but I was wondering if you knew anything about it."

I didn't know what to say. I wasn't sure if I should tell him George had shown me the private stash under the bricks in the shed, or if he was talking about a completely different stash of money.

"I didn't take anything," I said.

"I'm not saying you did. I mean, I don't want you thinking I'm accusing you of taking it. I was just wondering if you knew anything about it? I haven't talked to Rosemary or George yet."

"I don't know," I said. "You can check all my stuff if you want. You can check my clothes or my stuff in the bedroom."

He leaned forward and pinched the bridge of his nose. He seemed frustrated. I was worried and I hadn't even done anything.

"I'm sorry, Sequoyah," he said. "I know you didn't take anything. Don't think I think you did. I realize how bad this looks on me as a person. I like to talk to people without accusations. I apologize for asking."

"No problem," I said.

He crossed his legs and took another drag from his cigarette. Smoke streamed from his nostrils.

"I know what it's like to live in a strange place," he said. "When I was a kid my dad was murdered up north. A man he had planned to meet in the middle of the night pulled up in a car. It was snowing and the man demanded money. Two shots were fired and my father fell face-forward onto the road. They eventually caught the guy, but throughout childhood I kept replaying that murder over and over in my mind."

He was looking at the cigarette in his hand.

"My dad was a bootlegger," he said. "I imagined it happened like this: the killer lit a cigarette, then got into his car and drove away while snow fell on Dad's dead body. That's how I saw it. Then I moved in with my aunt Alice, who was patient enough to deal with me. It took some time but everything worked out in the end. My dad, he always took me to the horse races. He taught me to look at speed index, weight, class, whether the horse was on Lasix or not, whether the jockey was any good, whether the trainer was any good, and how much money the horse was running for. At some point I got good at handicapping six-furlong thoroughbred races, which was easier than betting on quarter horses."

"I want to go sometime," I said.

"Thoroughbreds are more fun to bet on," he told me. "Long shots are less likely to do anything in quarter horse races. Too many low odds."

I didn't know what to say, but it felt like Harold was being honest with me, or at least trying to be. Maybe he felt guilty about his secret life as a bookie, spending all that time setting point spreads to get the edge in a wager. He stared at me in the darkness, cigarette in mouth, smoke hanging around his head like he was burning to death.

GEORGE SEEMED TO HAVE calmed down when I went to bed. He was sitting on his bed in the dark, wearing a clip-on tie and slacks. He turned on the lamp and started talking.

"My tie is crooked and at an angle for a reason," he said. "It means I'm a hard worker. It means I've had to loosen my tie due to stress and a strong work ethic. Work ethic is important. Work hard and make money. Save, invest. Buy low and sell high. Work, sir. Work. Do you want to know what I've gotten done today? I finished a budget for Harold and Agnes. I've written nine pages of my novel. I've made a grocery list for Agnes since she always goes to the grocery store and realizes she's forgotten the list. I wrote a list of long-term goals to achieve before I'm twenty so that I won't have to be a fry cook or panhandler."

"Are you scared of me?" I said.

"I was worried you were going to kill me," he said. "I thought you cut my lip or something to make it bleed."

He sat slumped like a beaten dog. I was still new in the house. He was still trying to figure me out. My face, the scars. My unwillingness to talk about my past with him. He knew almost nothing about me, and I knew very little about him.

"I won't kill you," I said. "Maybe I'll take a knife and hack up your face like mine. Right?"

He looked at me. "I need a briefcase. I can carry my novel in it now that it's getting bigger."

He reached into the drawer beside his bed and retrieved a letter. He unfolded it and held it up for me to take. "This came today," he said. "You can read it if you want."

I went over and took it. I read it silently while standing in front of him. The letter was written in cursive, in blue ink, on hotel stationery.

Dear George,

I hope everything's going well for you. We hope you had a good Christmas. Your Grandpa and I are currently on

*vacation in Las Vegas. Our food here at the Frontier Hotel
is delicious. Last night we ate dinner at a seafood restaurant. We had salmon mousse on cucumber slices. Grandpa
tried sushi for the first time. He said his was delicious.
Mine wasn't so good. I drank a Perrier with my meal.
Tonight we might try an Italian restaurant that has good
minestrone. Or maybe we'll try a steak house here in the
hotel. I'm sure the food will be delicious. We already checked
the menu. Grandpa's sweet tooth may give in for dessert
tonight. Chocolate mousse and coffee sounds good. Take care.*

Grandpa and Grandma

"Your grandparents?" I asked.

"Yeah."

"Do they write you lots of letters?"

"No. They wrote three years ago when they were in
Florida. They don't call. They don't really write letters much
except to talk about food. They wouldn't let me live with
them."

He scratched at the back of his neck. I waited for him to
say something else, but he was silent in the dark.

"I once got a boy to believe I was a werewolf," I said.

He looked up at me.

"I'm serious," I said. "It was when I was at the shelter. The
kid was a real dumbshit. He was from some stupid shitty little
town. He kept putting his shoes on the wrong feet. He had
bad eyesight or something and wore thick glasses. Once he

asked me about my burn marks and I told him I was attacked by a wolf in the woods in the middle of the night. And I told him sometimes I wake up in the mornings naked with scratches and blood and mud all over my body. I told him other wolves gave me a hard-on. He stayed away from me."

George seemed to like this story.

"Here's another," I said. "I cut his hand with a pair of scissors and told him I didn't mean to because I sometimes have uncontrollable urges, and he believed me. He was a dumbshit, see? I told him I stole a pickup truck from a rodeo parking lot and drove it all the way down to Galveston, Texas, and that they had to bring me back in the back of a van with adult inmates. I told him they threw me down and handcuffed me just off the freeway. I told him a coyote came out of the brush and started to attack the trooper, ripped into him. Bit his leg so that blood sprayed everywhere. The coyote smelled my blood, knew I was part wolf. The coyote ripped out the trooper's organs and we started eating it. The kid believed every word."

"You ever drive a truck, really?" George asked.

"No."

"Me either," he said. He told me he was afraid of learning to drive because he would have an involuntary reaction to the stress and swerve into oncoming traffic.

"How do you know?" I asked. "You've never driven, so it doesn't seem likely."

"It's a fear I've always had," he said. "I see myself driving on an old highway at night. I mean one of the old highways with only two lanes, like the kind you see around here. I see headlights coming at me. Each passing set of headlights makes it worse."

"Makes what worse?"

"The involuntary jerk of the steering wheel. Turning directly into oncoming traffic and crashing. Dying instantly in a head-on collision. I don't know why."

He took a deep breath and stared at the wall.

All Thursday morning, the day of my mother's court hearing, I felt disoriented and lost, like the day of a funeral of someone close. Liz told me to dress nicely. Agnes helped me pick out a nice pair of pants and a button-up collared shirt. Rosemary was distant that morning. Downstairs, I told her my mother's probation hearing had me worried, but she didn't look concerned. She was sitting at the kitchen table, writing something in a notebook.

"I'm sure it'll be fine," she said.

"I guess I'm worried," I said.

"Don't worry, Sequoyah."

She was concentrated on whatever she was writing, but I didn't ask her about it. I listened to her breathing and found myself imagining she was in a cage and I was an observer who could free her. The cage I imagined was a glass cage with a glass door, and I had the key to set her free. Somehow the image felt absurd as I stood there watching her write in her notebook, but I couldn't help feeling I wanted her to look at me and say something. She was too invested in the letter or note or whatever she was writing to look up. I turned and walked away.

Liz showed up just after eight. The hearing was at ten-thirty, and we had to drive to Tulsa. On the drive we talked about school, and she asked me whether I liked living with the Troutts, those sorts of things. She wasn't bringing up my mother, and neither was I, but the subject hung there between us, silent. Maybe we were both afraid to bring it up. And something about the morning felt off, as I remember it, possibly because of the dreary weather, the gray sky, a freezing winter day.

It was raining when we got to the courthouse in down-town Tulsa. Inside, I was able to meet with my mother before the hearing. They brought her into a room, where I sat with Liz. I was irritated by everything there—all the people in the courthouse, the procedures, the deputy's mean stare. She had gotten thin since I'd visited her last, and her hair was longer and pulled back. Her eyes were bloodshot. But worse than that, it occurred to me how much she had lost her freedom. She wasn't able to have a private conversation with her own son, not until a court of law allowed it. The deputy scratched at his crew cut and stood with his arms crossed.

"You won't come see me when I get out, will you?" she said. "You won't come see me or miss me. You won't have anything to do with me."

"That's not true," I said.

"You look nice. Is the family you're staying with treating you good?"

"I like them."

My mother looked at Liz, as if for confirmation.

"They like Sequoyah," Liz spoke up. "They're nice people."

"It's important to be with good people," she said. "If they don't let me go I want you to keep coming to visit."

"I will."

She leaned in. "You won't come see me," she said again.

"Stop saying that. I need to tell you about what I've been doing."

She listened, and I knew from then on that she would listen to me the way I'd always listened to her. I told her about Harold and Agnes Troutt and their house in the country. I told her about George and Rosemary and the new school I attended.

"It's better than anywhere I've stayed," I told her. "The country is like being back in Cherokee County."

I saw the look of tenderness on her face, and I knew she was happy that I was in a good, safe place. It struck me then how strong grief and hope were. Grief and hope were our anchor, holding us together. I wouldn't let grief tear us apart, and I knew my mother didn't want that either. When she leaned forward to hug me I almost cried. I don't really know why—maybe I realized right then how much I'd missed her, or maybe I clung to some sort of hope that we could be together, just the two of us, the way it was before. Yet somehow I knew that wouldn't be a possibility.

"Your hair looks nice," she told me. "Whatever you do, don't cut it."

In the courtroom they wouldn't let me sit at the table with my mom, so I had to sit with Liz in the public seating. There wasn't anyone else with us. Liz took my hand and held it, something she had never done before. I should've known then. I think she already knew what was going to happen. I sat forward when they brought my mother into the room. She was handcuffed and wearing an orange jumpsuit. She stood with her attorney in front of the judge, who was reading something.

Because it was her second conviction, and because her charge was intent to distribute, she was denied probation and ordered to return to the state correctional facility. I watched them lead her out of the courtroom. She turned and looked at me, which destroyed me. I couldn't handle that look. It was as if all the grievances of my life overwhelmed me right then. After the attorneys and the court reporter left the room, Liz told me she would give me a minute to myself. I sat alone in the courtroom. It was freezing in there. I looked at the judge's bench and the witness stand and at the chairs where the jury members sat. I looked at the tall ceiling and the woodwork around the room. I wasn't sure what I felt in the courtroom, but it was no longer sadness, and it wasn't sympathy for my mother.

"I'm sorry," Liz said on the drive back.

"I'm fine," I said.

We passed old buildings through town, empty convenience

stores, gutted houses with weeds and tall grass growing. We drove under the overpass with graffiti sprayed in letters I couldn't make out. There was a woman walking along the side of the road with her three kids. She was carrying sacks of groceries while her kids trailed behind slowly, all of them staring at the ground while they walked. There were parts of town that reminded me of back home in Cherokee County, neighborhoods with cars parked in yards, trailers, pickups with tinted windows. We drove out of town and headed toward the countryside, driving into what felt like another part of the world, a place I was unfamiliar with. The land was low and flat, mostly farms, with barns and silos and fields stretching to the horizon.

"I'm fine," I said again.

WHEN LIZ DROPPED ME off back at the Troutts, I went upstairs to the attic to be by myself. I pulled off my shirt and lay down on the dusty floor. I couldn't bring myself to feel anything more. The whole day seemed empty. Up there in the attic I kept thinking about my mother standing in front of the judge with her head down. With my shirt off I fell asleep, and when I woke Harold was nudging me on the arm, asking me if I wanted to come down for dinner.

"I don't think so," I said.

"Or if you want to talk or anything," he said. "Agnes and I are here."

"I know."

Harold went back down, and I sat up and turned on the lamp. I heard a door shut downstairs. I heard footsteps on the hardwood floor. I was certain everyone wanted to leave me alone to grieve. The problem, though, was that I couldn't feel sad about what had happened, couldn't feel sad about my mother going away for a few more years. I'd grown accustomed to being away from her.

I decided I needed to go out for a walk. That afternoon the wind blew cold and heavy, in circular gusts. I left because I couldn't bear to sit in the house and feel sorry for myself. I needed to keep moving, to think about other things and walk around in the woods for a little while. With my coat on, I took the trail behind the house. I saw red-winged blackbirds gather at the windowsill as I left. I saw a red-tailed hawk return to its same nesting tree, in the blowing wind. Down the road, an amber pond with moss on the bank was full of catfish and largemouth bass. George told me he had seen bullfrogs and yellow-striped ribbon snakes there, along with muskrats swimming near the bank. As I walked through the woods I saw fog hanging over the trail ahead of me. I saw cedar waxwings with apple blossom petals in their beaks, watching me from their branch.

The air was heavy with the smell of dead things. As I walked I felt an increasing apprehension for my life and everything around me. I thought of my friend Eddie, who was homeless for a while back in Tulsa. He kept running away. I knew little of his home life. He'd joined up with a few others and they lived in and out of shelters, which was where I met him. When they were on the street they prostituted themselves, crept around the city at night, through winding tunnels, dark streets, sidling up on drunken old men and then rummaging through their wallets, prying up particle board and removing nails, anything they could find and use as weapons if they needed to. They weren't afraid of anything. I knew I could never be like that.

I thought I heard running water, but there was no water. I thought of my childhood in Cherokee County, when I was younger and playing in the Illinois River. I would make paper boats and float them down the river. I found strange toys there: pieces of a jigsaw puzzle and a plastic wind-up kangaroo that hopped. I found a broken music box and old tennis balls. I found a small miniature piano that didn't work regardless of how hard I banged on its keys. I remember wondering why people threw things away like this, or whether they set them free. The people who lived nearby must've thought the river would've somehow swallowed up all those objects and carried them away.

I walked down a trail, past trees with roots dug deep into the earth. Birds flew out of a scattering of trees, making noises. I gazed into the clouds, hoping for a sign, an answer, a signal, but nothing came.

THAT NIGHT, I WOKE to what sounded like a gasp or faint cry. I sat up in bed and looked over at George, who was still asleep. I wasn't sure whether there was really a sound or whether I dreamed it. I lay in bed for a moment with my arm over my eyes, but I felt restless. Thirsty, I got up and went downstairs to the kitchen, turned on the light and filled a glass of tap water. It was after three. The house was dark, dead silent.

From the kitchen window I could see the swing set out back, near the shed. I felt it calling to me in the moonlight. I found myself staring at it as I drank the water, thinking about a park I went to with my mother when I was little, a park far away from here. I thought about swinging high on that swing set, my mother pushing me from behind. When I finished the water I put the glass in the sink and slipped out the back screen door.

The swing set was outlined in a strange armature of blue light. Outside in the elements of the winter night, I was drowsy and sensitive to everything around me: the moonlight, the chill, the rustle of trees in the wind, the vast darkness that stretched past the yard into the woods. I sat on the cold seat of the swing and gripped the chains, where a fringe of frost gathered and made my hands even colder. Slowly I began swinging myself back and forth, kicking my feet as I swung higher and higher, and soon I was swinging as high as I could. The swing was squeaking and my head buzzed.

I'm not sure how long I kept swinging that night, but thinking back it seems like only an instant. I remember feeling overwhelmed with joy and secrecy, as if the whole world was asleep, and I was alone in the country, the only person, elated. When I came to a stop, I walked through the yard drowsily and slipped back inside. I locked the sliding door and quietly made my way upstairs, stepping lightly through the hall and back into my room, where George was still sleeping with his mouth open. I walked over to him and looked down at him. He was sleeping really heavily, I could tell. I wanted him to jolt awake and felt a strange thrill at the thought of scratching him or grinding my thumb into his face. I started to reach for his mouth but stopped myself.

Back in my bed, I breathed heavily and my heart raced. Soon I grew sleepy again. I saw a grainy shape flash across the ceiling. I saw patterns of light that looked like small children dancing on the dark walls.

THE NEXT DAY WHEN George and I returned home from school, Agnes was sitting on the couch. "Rosemary's not home," she said. "She hasn't come home and she doesn't work today."

"Do you have her work schedule?" George asked.

"I know she doesn't work on Wednesdays."

We were all silent a moment, and I could tell they were both worried. "It could be trouble," George said. "But maybe not. But probably so."

"It's nothing to worry about right now," Agnes said. "We had an argument. Actually, she and Harold had an argument. It doesn't matter what it was about."

"Maybe she's in the woods drawing," George said.

"Maybe. I don't know. I shouldn't have said anything, I guess."

"We'll go to the woods," I said.

"Follow the trail north if you go," Agnes said. "George knows where it is. I know she walks that way sometimes. She has before."

"North," I said.

"The trails lead down a hill. She goes down there to paint sometimes. You have to be careful if you're with George."

I looked at George, who was rocking back and forth, nervous. I was damaged in spirit, more so than George. I could tell he didn't want to go. It was freezing outside, but nothing was coming down and there was still plenty of daylight left.

"George gets nervous in the woods," Agnes said. "But you need to go, George, and see if you can find Rosemary."

He agreed, and after he put on his coat, George and I went out and walked north from the house, past the creek and into the woods, through the fierce cold wind. The trees around us were silent and motionless. George lagged behind, stopping for a moment to brace himself against the bark of a tree, and I had to turn around and go back to him.

"What's wrong?" I asked. "You're too cold? It isn't so bad."

"It's not the cold," he said. "It's just that maybe I should wait here while you go on."

"Why?"

"I don't like the hill ahead. I don't go down it."

He looked frightened all of a sudden. He stood with his back to the tree, his hands stuffed in the pockets of his coat.

I didn't keep questioning it. I'd learned soon enough not to keep questioning such things with George.

So I walked on, through the trees, and followed the hill until I realized there was another hill across the way that was too steep for me to try to climb. All around me were twisting branches, dead brush, patches of old snow on the ground. I knelt down and took a cigarette from my coat. There was movement nearby and my heart jumped. A rabbit ran away. I lit the cigarette and exhaled a long mixture of smoke and cold air. I smoked the cigarette and thought about what I was doing, sitting alone at the bottom of a hill in the woods, looking for Rosemary. Why had it come to this, after all, as though her life depended on my saving her from something or someone? What was I doing here?

I flicked the cigarette into the dirt and started back up the hill I'd just come down. Sunlight streamed down through massive trees. In the cold wind I trudged through the brush until I saw George standing at the same tree. When he saw me he started waving his arm. I waved back. Once I reached him he told me he'd heard a voice calling his name and asked if it was mine.

"It sounded like it came from far away," he said. His mouth was quivering from the cold. "I wasn't sure, I thought it was you."

"It wasn't me," I said. "You're sure you heard someone calling your name?"

"They called my name."

"Maybe it was the devil," I said. I leaned down and picked

up a stick. Then I threw it to the ground and started stomping on it with my foot.

George seemed frightened, even more than before. He stepped away from me, his shoes crunching in the twigs and brush, and slowly his expression changed and I saw tears gather in his eyes. I wasn't sure what was happening. I didn't know whether I should try to cheer him up or calm him down. He stepped backward, watching me. The silence hung there in the air before us, when I suddenly realized George was afraid of me.

"Let me go home," he said.

"All right," I said. "All right, we'll walk back to the house."

But he pulled himself further into his coat, lowering his head, stepping backward until he fell and cowered against the gnarled, twisted root of a tree. I was afraid he would start screaming.

"It's okay," I told him. "Everything's fine. Hey, George, let's go back to the house."

He wouldn't move. He remained in this position, not looking at me as I tried to talk to him. Soon I gave up and sat down across from him. We sat there for half an hour.

Finally we heard footsteps crunching and Agnes arrived. She was able to calm George down enough so that he could stand and walk back to the house. I wasn't sure what had happened, but I explained everything to Agnes on the walk back.

When we arrived back inside, Rosemary was still gone.

That night it took an hour for Agnes to calm George's anxiety about going into the woods. I had no idea he would be so shaken by it, but Agnes was patient about trying to help me understand.

"You can't take it personally," she said. "There are some things in his past that can be triggered. It doesn't matter now, of course. But it's good for all of us to know for future reference. It's not anyone's fault."

George was sitting cross-legged on the floor by the fireplace, wrapped in an afghan. He rocked back and forth as though swaying to slow music in his head. I apologized to everyone. I didn't even know what I was apologizing for, but my head was hurting and I needed to be by myself, which is what I told them.

"You didn't do anything wrong," Agnes said.

I asked not to be disturbed and went upstairs to be alone in my room. I stopped at Rosemary's door in the hall and picked the lock. I already had a story that I was looking for a specific drawing she did in case someone came upstairs and caught me. I went to her closet, where there was hosiery on the floor. I picked up a pair of black hose, wadded it up and slipped it into my pocket. I don't recall why, exactly, I did this—I knew I wouldn't wear it; maybe I wanted to keep an article of her clothing close to me, and a pair of hose seemed arbitrary enough that maybe she wouldn't miss it, like a dirty sock.

I pulled off my T-shirt, then my pants. I stood in her closet in my underwear, running my hands over her clothes: her skirts and jeans, her shirts, her sweaters and jackets. In the closet mirror I saw myself standing there, thin as a rail, the burns on my face swelled in the reflection like a bad disease. I was not attractive, was neither handsome nor charming in any way. Had I tried on any of her clothes I would've been disappointed, because I would never have a body like Rosemary's.

Standing there, I considered pulling all her clothes from their hangers and covering myself with them like blankets. I wanted to sleep on the floor of her closet, among the clothes and shoes and tiny boxes and loose hangers on the floor. Such a small space brought safety, comfort. I recall a few things specific to this moment. I recall the dizzying atmosphere in the space, how beautiful and isolated and psychedelic it all felt, as if I were living inside the body of Ziggy Stardust or some obscure coke-snorting, heroin-shooting glam rock star from the seventies. I recall the urge to vomit and thrust myself into the wall. I recall the desire to become someone else completely. I wanted to put on those clothes, then immediately had an impulse to tear them from the hangers and rip them to shreds, stretch the fabric and stomp on them like fire. I felt high, but I wasn't high. Slowly, then, I pulled on my shirt and jeans. I left the room, locking the door as I closed it.

That night we stayed up late waiting for Rosemary to come home. At almost midnight, as I was going to bed, I asked George why Harold and Agnes didn't call the police.

"She's left before," he said. "It happened once last year. She left for a day and came back. Maybe they think she'll be back tomorrow."

I wished I knew what she was going through. It was all so confusing back then. That night I dreamt of my mother, whose hands were cold and shaking as she lifted vegetables from the sink. In my dream I stood in the Troutts' kitchen, watching my mother clean vegetables and wash dishes with a sponge. Neither of us spoke. I looked at an open window, where a flock of blackbirds flew in and perched themselves all around the room—on the curtain rod, on lamps, on the TV set—and I remember watching them as they preened themselves; it was as if something bad was about to happen.

"Any second now the windows will shatter," my mother said without looking up.

In the dream I was unable to speak. Immediately, I began separating the silverware on the kitchen counter. I felt a sense of urgency to separate, one by one, each fork, knife, and spoon. At this point my mother reached for one of the forks and held it out in front of her like a relic, as if it were a work of art she'd created.

• • •

THE NEXT DAY, LIZ called on the phone and asked how I was doing. I told her about Rosemary leaving and how we hadn't heard from her.

"Sounds like she needs help," Liz said. "Does her caseworker know?"

"I think so," I said. "I'm sure Harold and Agnes called her. But it's only been a day. It's just weird that we haven't heard from her."

"That's not like her, right?"

"Right."

"You're worried about her," she said. "But that's understandable since you've become so close to her. She's your friend, someone to talk to. She means a lot to you, right? So it doesn't make any sense why she wouldn't try to contact you."

"I'm starting to wonder if something bad happened," I said. "I don't know what to think."

"Make sure her caseworker knows about it. Maybe the police should know. Has anyone called them?"

"I don't think so. I'm not sure."

"Go talk to Harold and Agnes about it."

Agnes drove us to Nora's house to see if she was there. We got out of the car and stood looking at the old house, which appeared to be empty and deserted. Trees cast shadows along the street. As we approached their front porch I noticed the rosebushes and thought of Nora falling from the second-story window into them. I had an image of her falling, arms outstretched, tumbling into the bushes, knocked unconscious by the impact. In my mind's eye Nora seemed so empty, so lifeless. Wind chimes rang solemnly with a gust of wind as we waited at the door after ringing the bell. We waited and waited and no one answered.

"I don't even know Nora's parents," Agnes said. "How do I not know them? How has this happened?"

We drove to Farah's house across the railroad tracks on the west side of town. Farah came to the door wearing black lipstick and a Cure T-shirt.

"I haven't talked to her since last week," she told us.

"You don't know where she could be?" Agnes asked.

"She could be anywhere," Farah said. "Have you talked to Nora? What about V.J.?"

"Who's V.J.?"

"Oh," Farah said. "Oh, he's a guy who plays in a band. I don't know him. I don't know how to get in touch with him. Sorry."

"Can you call me if you hear anything?" Agnes said.

"Sure," she said. "Sure, no problem. Good luck."

We drove to the CD Sound Mart, where Rosemary sometimes liked to shop for music. We drove to the lake. We drove to the East Side Mall and asked the girl who worked at the Orange Julius, another friend Rosemary had mentioned. We looked in clothing stores, in shoe stores, in bookstores. We couldn't find her anywhere in the mall.

"Someday technology will make it easier to find people," George said as we rode down the escalator.

"That's not likely to happen in our lifetime," Agnes said.

As we passed the movie theatre, I saw a poster for *Rain Man*, starring Dustin Hoffman and Tom Cruise, and I remembered seeing on the local news that parts of it were filmed in Oklahoma the previous year. "There's that movie that was filmed in Oklahoma last summer," I said. "Guthrie or El Reno or somewhere."

Agnes and George both looked at the poster as we walked past.

"Tom Cruise sucks," George said, staring straight ahead.

After we got back home, when George went upstairs, I told Agnes about the secret place in the woods where Rosemary had taken me on our bicycles.

"Where is it?" she asked. "Can you take us there?"

"I don't know, I followed her that day and didn't pay much attention. I can try."

"We have to try," she said.

When Agnes called for George he decided he would stay there, too tired from all the searching, so it was only Agnes and I in her car. We drove slowly down Comanche Road, down the hill as I looked out the window, trying to find places that looked familiar. All the woods looked the same to me. I saw no clearings, no familiar trails. Then I noticed the low-hanging branch with the pink bandanna tied to it, and I told Agnes to stop.

"It's here," I said, pointing to the trail through the woods.

She pulled over to the side of the road and looked. "Are you sure?"

"This is it. I remember the bandanna in the tree. That's her mark. We have to walk a little ways though."

"It'll be dark soon," Agnes said. "How far is it?"

"It shouldn't take long."

We got out of the car and started down the trail. Leaves crunched as we walked, and I found myself walking ahead of Agnes, who walked slowly anyway. I tried not to think about wildlife roaming around, though I knew in the back of my mind they were there, coyotes and bobcats and snakes. I tried to remain focused and alert, a protector to Agnes and even, possibly, Rosemary. We came to the fork in the road and I remembered we had turned left.

"It's right up here," I said, Agnes following behind. I heard crackling noises from her steps and grew worried. I couldn't see Rosemary anywhere. We came upon the area near the small hill that sloped down to the creek, and there was no sign of anyone.

"This is the spot," I said.

Agnes called out for Rosemary then, which made the woods come alive. I thought I heard sounds from the trees, wind in leaves, the crackle of leaves and branches from small, frightened animals. I hurried to the slope and looked down at the creek, but Rosemary wasn't there.

"Rosemary!" Agnes called again. We stood in the dim

woods, feeling ridiculous, as if she would suddenly appear from under a blanket of leaves, or jump out from behind a tree and laugh at us. That's how it felt, as if everything were merely a game of hide-and-seek, some prank she'd decided to pull. Yet we both knew this was no game.

"She's not here," Agnes said. "We better head back before it gets dark."

We started back, and this time I walked slower, beside Agnes. I thought I saw something dark move in the trees but I didn't say anything. My mind has always been susceptible to brief flashes of light at night, or movement in dark places. I don't know how many nights I've started to drift off to sleep only to be awakened by some movement in the room, something that dropped from the ceiling or darted across the wall. I've never been able to pinpoint whether these things are real or imagined, or what, exactly, it means. As we walked back along the trail that evening, as the sun leaned west and the woods grew darker, I saw things like that, movement in the trees.

"It's getting dark," I said, but Agnes didn't answer, and I knew she was deep in thought about what was happening to Rosemary. I assumed she was more afraid than she was letting on.

When we got back home, Harold was standing on the porch. We hoped he had good news.

"She's not back," he said as we got out of the car.

"You haven't heard anything?" Agnes asked.

"Nothing."

"Did anyone even call?"

"No."

We went inside where it was warm. Agnes made hot chocolate and we all sat at the kitchen table. Harold took a sip and told me he was proud of me.

"You've shown a lot of courage," he said. "Taking the time to help look for Rosemary. That's a good thing. Are your headaches any better?"

"Not really," I said.

"Maybe we should have the doctor check it out," he said.

He looked out the window. We all sat quietly at the table, sipping our hot chocolate and staring out the window into darkness.

THE NEXT MORNING AGNES told us Rosemary's social worker had informed the police, and that they were out looking for her as well. I went to school afraid and nauseated all day, waiting for classes to end so I could get out of there. When the school day ended I ditched the bus and walked downtown in the rain. I hurried down Main until I reached the thrift store where Rosemary worked, hoping to find her, to talk to her, to see her—but she wasn't there. A woman working told me she hadn't seen her since last week. "She missed work the last two days," she said. "Is she missing?"

"I don't know," I said.

"Well, she needs to call me if you see her," the woman said.

"She needs to call me as soon as possible if she wants to keep working here."

My head was beginning to hurt. I felt like I was going to vomit and stepped outside, where it was raining harder. I leaned over and took a deep breath. I stood under the awning, unsure what to do. I thought about whether I should call Agnes or wait it out. Then a car pulled up in front of me and the driver rolled his window down. I couldn't tell who it was from the rain, but he called my name.

"Sequoyah," he yelled from the window, waving his arm. "Come on."

I rushed over to the car in the pouring rain and opened the passenger's side door. It was Jack, the man with the dog from down the street. The man with the hat, the man I had seen in the supermarket.

"Get in," he said.

I got into his car and closed the door. I was wet and a little confused, but he was laughing.

"You're awfully wet," he said. "I'm Jack, remember me?"

"Yeah."

"Need a ride? What's going on?"

I sort of shrugged. "Looking for someone," I said.

He seemed charmed by my reluctance to talk. In truth, he made me nervous. I wasn't threatened by him out of fear for my life, but his interest in me was not unlike the men who would ask me for rides when I would walk along Highway 30 back in Cherokee County.

We sat in the car while rain blurred the windshield. I didn't say anything or look over at him, but I didn't want to run away either.

"You're quiet," he said, and started to back out of the lot. "So, how's it going?"

"Fine, I guess."

"So, where do you live? I'll give you a ride home."

"Out in the country."

"With your parents?"

"Foster family, the Troutts."

"Harold Troutt?"

"Yeah, you know him?"

"I knew his father, Max Troutt," he said. "You know Harold's a bookie, right? Max Troutt ran a little gambling hub on the outskirts of town back in the fifties."

"I think Harold told me he was a bootlegger."

"Right," he said. "Right, he was a bootlegger. He was a friend of my uncle's. I liked him a lot. When I was a kid he taught me how to hit a golf ball. He showed me his clubs and explained the difference between irons and woods, a hook and a slice. He showed us how to grip a club. We couldn't afford our own golf clubs, but he had some old junior clubs. He always told me there was a certain grace in a good golf swing. It involved timing, balance, slowness. It involved patience. I watched him put on his golf shoes. We watched him tee up and stand over the ball with a driver. He shifted his balance from foot to foot. He made it look so easy. When he hit the ball, sometimes the tee flew out of the ground and landed in front of his feet."

It occurred to me I hadn't given him the address. He put on his blinker and pulled into a Sonic Drive-In.

"You want a drink?" he asked. "It's on me. Do you like Cherry Cokes?"

"Sure."

He rolled down his window and pushed the button on the OrderMatic. He ordered us both Cherry Cokes. He looked at me, then stared straight ahead. I saw the ring on his pinkie finger. I saw his hairless hands.

"So what do you do?" I asked.

"I was in advertising for a while in Chicago. My parents passed and I moved back. That's it. That's my whole story. What about you? What grade are you in?"

I looked out the window. The rain had let up and a gathering of grackles were walking around the parking lot, looking for food.

"Ninth," I said.

"Only a few years left of school," he said. "You're practically done."

The carhop, a girl I thought I recognized from school, brought our drinks, and Jack paid her.

"Harold's dad was a good guy," he said, handing me my drink. "I remember he became obsessed with catching the ferruginous hawk, which was rumored to be some three feet long with a wingspan of six feet. Do you know about the ferruginous hawk?"

"No."

"You don't know the story? Harold didn't tell you?"

"No."

"People in town were fascinated by the ferruginous hawk," he said. "It was a long time ago. Everyone wanted to kill it. The hawk swooped down and killed babies. It clawed kids by their hair and carried them away."

"A hawk," I said.

"A ferruginous hawk."

I thought about this.

"One night," he said, "some of Max's gambling buddies sat at the bar in the basement of the White Antelope Inn, where illegal slot machines and poker games were held, and discussed hunting the bird. Max wanted the bird badly. Four years earlier it had attacked his daughter, Harold's sister, when she was only six. The hawk swooped down and dug its claws into her scalp."

I crunched the ice with my straw.

"So they drove twelve miles out of town on County Road 9, turned north and took a gravel road overhung with branches a few miles until they reached a pasture near the woodsy Catoosa Creek area. Once they parked, they climbed a split rail fence and walked through thick pasture until they made it to the trees. They walked with their shotguns, searching for that hawk. They hunted all morning for it but never found it. I think around this time was when Harold started booking."

I drank my Cherry Coke and kept pushing the ice with the straw. There was too much ice.

"Isn't that a creepy story?" he asked.

"I don't know. Not really."

"Do you trust Harold?"

The question came out of nowhere, surprising me. I glanced at Jack and then looked away.

"I guess so," I said.

Driving with one hand on the wheel, he started searching his pockets with the other. "Oh damn," he said. "Damn, I forgot my nitroglycerine tablets. I have a heart problem. See, that's what happens when you hit fifty, Sequoyah. Do you mind if we stop by my apartment? I just live in south downtown. I live there with my dog. Then I'll take you home."

"No problem," I said.

He backed out of the Sonic parking lot and pulled away. We drove down Raider Street, past the used car dealerships and old cafés. There was a man on the street corner holding a bicycle wheel. He stared at me as we drove by.

Jack turned up the radio, some sort of old country music. "I have some friends staying with me," he said, tapping the steering wheel with his ring. "You should come in and meet them."

He lived in a building off Main Street, near the refinery in south downtown. He parked in front of his building, and I followed him upstairs. His apartment was dim but unusually spacious for a man who lived alone. When we walked in, there were other kids there. Jack told me to make myself at home. I watched him walk into a room, maybe the bedroom, and he closed the door.

I saw a boy lying on the couch. He yawned and rolled over, facing the back of the couch. There were two other boys sitting on the floor. They were playing a board game of some sort. One of the boys was wearing fingerless gloves, the other had his shirt off. Neither of them said anything, too focused on their game, staring down at the board between them. One of the boys rolled dice and moved a plastic piece along the board. The other stared at the board with his fingers on his temples, studying. Above, the ceiling fan hummed, the only sound in the room.

I stood quiet in the entryway. The walls were white and covered with framed pictures and paintings. The floor was hardwood with only a single rug near the window across the room. The two boys played their game quietly. Near the kitchen I saw a girl sitting on the floor with her head down. She was so silent I almost didn't see her. She might've been praying. She never looked up, never even moved. Maybe she was sleeping. Her hair was long and straight and hung down in front, so I wasn't able to see her face. I heard Jack's dog barking from another room.

The boy on the couch coughed in his sleep, hoarse and rich with phlegm, and out of nowhere I started to feel nauseated again. Before Jack returned, I slipped out the door and headed downstairs quickly. I left the building and hurried down the dark street, then I broke into a run, past the slumbering old buildings and cloudy windows. Cold, moldy air rose around me, heavy in my lungs, and I kept running until I was out of breath.

South downtown at night was dead, full of abandoned buildings, pale walls, and empty rooms. Once I was far enough away from Jack's apartment, I started looking for a pay phone. I walked past the old stores with "For Rent" signs in them, crossing to a parking lot on the other side. As I crossed, a man pulled up in a car beside me and rolled down his window. "Hey," he said. "Hey, where are you going?" I didn't look at him and kept walking with my hands in my pockets. I broke into a run across the parking lot and heard him calling after me, "Hey, where are you going?"

Darkness thickened around me as I headed down a residential street with cars parked along the curb in front of a house. It seemed a party was going on. Some people were standing outside on the porch, smoking. What was the occasion for a party in the middle of the week? I could hear a train in the distance. Farther down the street I heard a woman cry out. She was trying to help an old man from a car to a house, but the man had slipped and fallen, and now the woman was kneeling down to him. I hurried over to her and asked if I could help.

The woman turned to look at me, startled or frustrated, but when she saw that I was a kid she said, "Yes, please."

I put my hands underneath the man and helped her sit him up. The old man didn't seem to register his surroundings.

"He has dementia," the young woman said. "It's okay. If you can wait here for a minute I'll go to the front door and call for my husband."

"Okay, okay," I said, still holding the man so he wouldn't fall.

The woman stood and hurried to the porch. She opened the front door and called for her husband, who came out and helped lift the old man to his feet. The old man mumbled something, but I couldn't understand him. He had unkempt white hair and was wearing a coat and scarf.

"Let's get him inside," the woman's husband said, and we walked him to the porch, where the woman was holding the door open for us. We led the old man inside and helped him take off his coat and scarf, then sat him on the couch. Throughout all this, the man mostly remained silent, clenching his jaw every so often but never seeming angry or afraid.

"Thanks for your help," the woman's husband said. "He's gotten worse lately."

"Daddy?" the woman said to the old man. "Everything's all right?"

The old man nodded and started picking at something on his hand.

I could tell the husband and wife were staring at my face. "We appreciate your help," the husband said. "Do you live in the neighborhood?"

"No, I was at a party. I was at a friend's house," I said. "It was nothing really. I'm going home."

"Would you like something to drink?" the wife asked. "Tom, get him a pop. Do you want a pop?"

"Sure," I said.

I followed Tom into the kitchen. On the walls was thick wallpaper with flowery designs and ovals and rectangles where pictures once hung. The place was a mess: dirty dishes piled in the sink, spilled coffee, vials and prescription bottles of pills on the counter. In front of the prescription bottles were small paper cups, each filled with pills. "His medicine," Tom said. He squinted at them. "He takes six different kinds of pills," he said, "just to keep from having another stroke."

He opened the refrigerator and handed me a can of pop, which I opened. I thanked him.

"No problem at all," he said. "We appreciate your help. My father-in-law is really going downhill fast. He liked to talk about the Korean War and used to build sheds with his own hands. Poor guy can't do anything anymore."

I imagined his sleepless nights, lying on a hard bed with no sheets or pillows, unsettled thoughts racing through his mind. Alone, with no help, enduring the pain of the elderly, the back and knee aches, the bad dreams, difficulty breathing. Mumbling to himself.

"Forty years ago he built this house," he told me. "He hauled lumber and erected strong beams. He built a solid roof and laid good floors. He devoted his life to this place. It's sad."

I followed him back into the living room, where his wife was now sitting.

"Where do you live?" she asked me. "Do you need a ride?"

"East of town, in the country," I said.

"Tom, give him a ride home," she said to her husband. She looked at me. "Tom can give you a ride."

"Sure," Tom said. "Let me get my keys."

"You don't have to," I said. "I can call someone to come pick me up."

"It's no problem," the woman said. "Thanks for stopping to help."

A few minutes later I was riding in the car with Tom. He was quiet most of the drive. He asked me a couple of typical questions, like what grade I was in and what I liked to do for fun. He turned on the radio and asked what kind of music I liked.

"Anything," I said.

"I can't take country music," he said. "Not even the old stuff. So many people love it, but it makes me depressed. All the songs sound the same to me."

"Yeah."

"All those songs about misery and whiskey."

He laughed at himself. He was pleasant as we headed out

of town, east toward the country. I kept thinking how nice he and his wife were, and so I asked if they had any kids.

"We have a little girl named Chelsea," he said. "She's four. She was in bed when you were there."

I directed him down the road toward the Troutt house. When we pulled into the drive I could see the light on in the living room, and I figured Harold and Agnes would be angry that I was coming in late.

I thanked Tom for giving me a ride. He gave me a thumbs up and told me to take care of myself. He was so friendly and charming I wanted to run away with him.

INSIDE THE HOUSE, GEORGE was sitting at the typewriter, hunched over, pecking at the keys with two fingers. He was alone in the room and never looked up when I entered.

"Where is everyone?" I asked.

He looked up at me, squinting. "Rosemary came back," he said. "They had a fight. You missed it. Where were you?"

"She's back? Is she okay?"

"Yeah, you missed it. Where were you?"

"Walking around town. Where is she? Where is everyone?"

"Agnes went to bed and Harold's downstairs in his office. There's chili for you in the kitchen if you're hungry. Agnes wanted me to tell you. Did you eat supper?"

I stood there a moment, unsure what to do. I was exhilarated that she was back.

"Should I go talk to her?" I said.

"I wouldn't go up there. They had a fight. It was bad. You missed it."

I thought about it and decided he was right. I took off my coat and hung it up. George followed me into the kitchen, where I heated up a bowl of a chili in the microwave. I sat at the table and he sat across from me. I put a fistful of crackers into my chili and listened to George talk about what had happened. Rosemary had come home drunk. She'd stolen money from Harold, a few hundred dollars. Harold called her social worker and threatened to call the police and have her arrested. There was yelling. I was glad I wasn't there. George seemed bothered by it.

He looked at me and said, "I cowered into the couch. All I could do was pull the afghan over me. It was happening right in front of me in the living room."

"You were scared."

"Don't say it like that."

"Like what?"

He looked away. "You sound like Rosemary."

"You were scared," I said again.

The chili wasn't very good, or maybe I wasn't hungry. I ate only a couple of crackers and poured a glass of ice water. I drank the whole glass and when I finished I got up and put the bowl in the sink. Then I went upstairs and George followed closely behind, neither of us speaking, our steps creaking on the hardwood floor of the quiet upstairs hallway. All the lights were off. Rosemary was sleeping, so I didn't wake her. I went into my room and lay down on the bed. George came in and sat on the bed, watching me for a moment, then said he wanted to go back downstairs to type more.

From the window, I watched the drizzle come down in the yellow glow from the house light. Time passed, thoughts came. I couldn't think of what to say to Rosemary. Minutes crept by. I heard Rosemary's voice in my head, instructing me to breathe slowly. Her voice came and went. Her voice was there. I heard her say my name and I wondered whether we were communicating on some higher level of consciousness. Maybe she was awake in her room, I remember thinking this, and we were talking through each other's minds, each other's thoughts, if such a thing were possible. Of course this was insanity. But of course it wasn't insanity. I marveled at the thought as I lay in the dark, my breathing steady, silent.

The next morning when I woke, she remained in her room. I went to school as usual, struggled through the long misery of another day, and when I returned home she was still in her room. She was like this for a couple of days. I thought: I'll leave her alone. She'll appreciate that. All of us left her alone to grieve, to mourn, be angry, or do whatever it was she needed to do by herself. She ate her meals in her room, took two-hour baths in the upstairs bathroom, and kept her door shut.

For three days she consumed my thoughts. Something strange was going on, and I felt completely distanced from whatever it was. For a while I wondered whether she wanted me to check on her, if her isolation might be a call for help. Late on the third night, I finally gave in and tapped lightly on her door. At first she didn't answer, but I kept tapping. "It's Sequoyah," I said quietly. "Can we talk? I want to talk to you."

I waited. Then I heard the floor creak from her footsteps and she opened the door slightly, peering out. She looked terrible. Her eyes were puffy, like she'd been crying. She looked exhausted, sick.

"Hey," I said. "Are you okay?"

"I can't talk," she said.

"Why not?"

"Don't take it personally. It's not you, Sequoyah. I just have all this shit I'm dealing with."

"What kind of shit?"

"Seriously," she said. "I can't talk. I'm going outside and I need to be alone."

"Outside? What for? Can I go with you?"

"No."

"Why not?"

She looked at me, and I could feel the pain in her stare. It was as if I was no longer anyone she wanted to be associated with.

"Why not?" I said again.

"Hang on," she said, and closed the door. I stood in the dark hallway waiting. I looked down at the floor. I looked back at the door. She took forever. Then, finally, she opened the door fully and stepped out. She was now dressed and wearing a dark jacket and white gloves.

"Fine," she said. "Fine, you can come if you want. Just be quiet about it."

I followed her downstairs, through the living room and out the back door. I didn't bother to put on a coat myself. Outside it was freezing, the wind blowing bitter cold. The moon was full with a ring of light that stretched into the dark sky around it. We walked through the yard, past the swing set to the shed. The dust as we entered powdered my throat. Rosemary turned on the light and knelt down to the floor, where she removed the bricks that hid Harold's money, but there was no money there.

"Where's all the cash?" I said. "He put it somewhere else?"

She didn't answer. She remained kneeling there in silence a moment before putting the bricks back. Then she stood, breathing heavy. She almost looked like she was sweating, which was odd since it was freezing in there. I stood with my arms crossed, shivering without a coat. I recall the way she was breathing, her look of wild abandonment.

"What's up," I said.

"Fuck," she said. "Fuck, fuck."

She turned off the light and left, and we were back outside again in the night. I saw tall black telephone poles stretching into the sky. I saw the willow tree in the distance, shadowy and monstrous. It occurred to me now how much Rosemary must've liked to abandon herself to danger, as she grasped a fallen branch that lay near the shed. I watched her pick it up and, for reasons not clear to me, begin clobbering it into the ground.

"Don't be so pissed off," I called out.

She hammered the branch harder. She gritted her teeth, her face frozen in anger.

"Goddamn it!" she screamed, and threw the branch down. She stomped on it with her boot, still gritting her teeth. She was livid. I'd never seen her so angry, and truthfully I found it a little bit exciting.

"Hey," I said, "Hey, what's wrong?"

She didn't answer me. She stomped and then stopped herself and rested, hunched forward. In the darkness I wondered whether she was crying. Even if she were, I knew she wouldn't let me see. So I gave her a minute while I stood there freezing.

"Let's go inside," I said.

"Yeah," she said, out of breath. "Yeah, all right, Sequoyah."

I remember my jaw was trembling from the cold while I waited for her to walk back to the house, and I followed like a dog, trailing behind.

Inside the house, where the blinds were closed and the long curtains covered the windows downstairs, the ceiling light was bright in the living room. Standing in the center of the room was Harold, in pajama pants and slippers, holding a flashlight.

"Where are you going?" he asked Rosemary.

"Upstairs."

"Wait a minute."

"Leave me alone," she said.

He was staring at her as she headed toward the stairs, but she wouldn't look at him.

"Shouldn't we talk, Rosemary? Don't you owe me that?"

She didn't answer.

"Rosemary," he said again, his voice sounding more hurt than angry.

I followed her upstairs, afraid to look at Harold.

In the hallway upstairs she glanced over her shoulder. "Why are you following me?"

I didn't answer, but I followed her anyway. And though she said she didn't want me in there, she didn't close the door on me, so I sat on her bed. In her room, her body looked shallow, almost frail in her white T-shirt. I sat with her in silence a long while, until she told me to leave.

"I don't want you here," she said.

"Why not?"

"It's not fair. They're taking me out of here. They're sending me back to rehab."

"No."

"There's not shit I can do about it," she said. "You can't say anything to help."

I thought for a moment. "I don't get what you mean."

"Sequoyah, just leave me alone. I don't like you anymore."

I thought I felt the light flicker, but I'm not sure it flickered. She got up and went into her closet while I crossed my arms and sat there, watching her. I wanted her to see my face. I wanted her to see a different, more masculine side of me when I got angry. All the time she had spent with me, all the things she said and the looks she gave me were concentrated in that moment. I bunched up the fabric of the comforter in my hands while she rooted in the closet. She was talking to herself, that I knew, then the light blinked out and the room fell dark except for the light from the closet, where she stood in the doorway, a shadowy figure.

"You never listen," she said, and these were her final words. In the dimly-lit room I couldn't tell if she was laughing or sobbing. A surge of anger struck me. It stopped me cold, seeing her standing there. I noticed the gun in her hand. Beyond that, I remember hearing a slight hum that seemed to vibrate from somewhere in the room. The vibration moved across the floor and entered me, my body, my mind. The vibration was its own malicious presence, some isolated entity that existed only in that moment. I knew I was not myself, and it felt stimulating and good. I was someone furious, someone hurt, someone blighted by infectious rage. A split second later I could not contain myself and sprang from the bed and placed my empty hand on her gun-gripping hand, my hand on her hand, and we held on, both confronting ourselves, both relentless.

A bright day with no wind, the sun reflecting in a blue sky, I took a nice walk alone down the side of the road, following the tracks of a coyote or large dog. I felt confused and yet strangely happy. I had a cryptic affinity for the unknown. The tracks held paw prints of some large beast I imagined wandering around at night, looking for smaller animals to devour. I heard the sounds of birds in the trees. In my pocket I kept a switchblade I'd swiped from a drawer in the downstairs cabinet, probably Harold's, in case I needed protection from the wildlife. My head was buzzing, and I felt the need to break into a run, down the road and through the trees, to rid myself of excess energy. I expected to quickly become popular, part of the family with the dead girl. It would be on the local TV news, in the newspapers, talked about all over town. I was part of this family, this story.

This would be historical, and my head buzzed from it. I felt dizzy.

They found Rosemary's suicide note, folded in thirds, on the dresser in her room. It was her handwriting, there was no question. She was dead. Dead, dead, dead. Nobody even suspected murder. Nobody had a serious motive. She had attempted suicide before, everyone knew this, so it was only a matter of time. She wasn't seeing her counselor despite telling her caseworker, Harold, and Agnes, that she was going every week. She was a liar.

"Maybe we gave her too much freedom," Agnes told the caseworker. "I don't know. I don't know. Maybe I could've been better."

"I can't believe it happened," the caseworker said.

"I can't describe anything I'm feeling," Harold said.

The night she died, long after the gunfire, after the police came and talked to me and everyone else, after Harold and Agnes went into their room and closed the door, I pulled off my shirt and crawled into George's bed with him. He was facing away from me, but he was awake. He let me put my arm around him. It was six in the morning and my heart was racing.

THOSE FIRST COUPLE OF nights I kept feeling dizzy. Late at night I took aspirin and slept two, three hours at most. Nobody was talking to anyone in the house. Nobody was talking at all. George retreated to his room, I stayed in the attic, which now felt more menacing and occupied, as if ghosts visited in my sleep. I dreamed of an old dead woman sitting in the rocking chair. I dreamed of hideous-looking dwarfs carving the organs out of a dead animal. I dreamed of falling out of windows. This went on for a few days while Agnes and Harold kept to themselves. The house, once full of anticipation and wonder, now felt silent, dead. We kept distant from the newspaper, people who called from the school, strangers who knew Rosemary. Who were these people, I wondered. There were strange men and women calling to offer condolences. Adults, teenagers. People I'd never seen brought flowers. The doorbell rang and soon we quit answering it.

I pretended to be sick on the day of her funeral. I forced myself to vomit in the kitchen so everyone at the table would hear me, rammed two fingers down my throat and choked myself. I gagged and eventually threw up on the floor. I'm not sure I tricked them, but it made me feel better, and I didn't want to go to the funeral. Agnes walked in, upset. I loosened my tie and lay on the cold tile, clutching my stomach. They were all worried about me.

While they were at the funeral I left the house and walked to an abandoned warehouse where homeless men slept. The place was full of broken bottles and trash. The windows were broken and tiny pieces of glass crunched under my feet. The walls were spray-painted with gang graffiti, giant swirly letters and weird designs. Strips of light slanted in from the cracks in the roof, and even though the homeless men sleeping there looked scary, none of them ever tried to touch me or harass me in any way. On the contrary, bored, I wanted to harass them. I was kicking around in the dirt and walked upstairs to the second or third floor of the warehouse, where it was empty. I stood at the window, watching an old guy march on the gravel below. He was crazy, thinking he was a general or something in the war. He had an unkempt beard and wore a green army cap. He wore an old army surplus jacket. He took a few steps and saluted. I tossed a crushed Dr Pepper can out the window so that it landed near where he was marching. He spun around quickly and raised his arms. He looked around, then took a few slow steps, observing his surroundings. He started marching again.

I crushed another can and tossed it. This one landed in front of him, stopping him so abruptly that his arms flailed as if he were describing something enormously round. He knelt down to the can, edged closer to it as if it were a bomb. He tapped it with the toe of his boot. Then he stood upright and placed his hand on his heart. From where I was watching above, I thought I could see his mouth moving, and I imagined him giving orders to an invisible army down there. Once or twice he yelled out like he was in pain. He lifted a finger and pointed to the sky as if observing airplanes. He spun around and marched, stomping his boots. I watched him stop walking and pull up his pants.

This went on for maybe twenty minutes. I kept throwing cans and he kept reacting, marching. I smoked a cigarette and sat by the window, watching him. Finally he walked away, through the weeds, and didn't return. From the window, I could hear him yelling as he marched.

. . .

THE LONG LIFE, I kept thinking later, this phrase Rosemary used. For several days after she was gone I thought of "long life." I thought of the word "life" and tried to define it in my mind. I thought of "mind." I repeated the phrase, "long life."

One afternoon there was a Native American man standing in his yard near the school. He stood with his arms crossed and his eyes closed. Who does this in their yard, standing there without moving? I watched him for a few minutes to see whether he was temporarily praying or what, maybe looking for some inward peace, an advanced form of meditation.

I stood across the street, watching him. His hair was long and white and he wore a pale sweater and blue jeans. His arms remained crossed, maybe he was waiting on someone. He looked peaceful, though, standing there with his eyes closed, and I thought of a movie I once saw with a man standing at the edge of a cliff, about to jump off to commit suicide and fall to his death, and there he stood, like this man, standing there with his eyes closed.

The bus arrived. I waited for the kids to get on and the driver to close the door. Nobody said anything to me as I stood there, waiting, and finally the bus droned away; and there was the man in the yard, still standing with his arms crossed and his eyes closed. I don't know why more people weren't paying attention to him. I wanted to be like him, to see something, to be able to draw inward, avoiding distraction.

Later that night I stood in Rosemary's room, looking at myself in the mirror. I pretended to stab myself in the neck, slicing my own throat, making dying faces. I did this nine times.

HER DEATH WAS FINAL, this is what I soon started to realize. I found myself sleeping less each night. The loss was beginning to sink in. The initial shock, such a strange sensation that had left me so confused, was now fading, and though I had only known her a short time, I'd never watched anyone die in front of me. My room had lost its identity, or maybe I had lost my identity, or maybe it was the lost connection to the room, the house, and everything inside. I stood by my bed each night, looking into the mirror. The way I saw myself was different than before, my face and body thin and weak in the scant light of the room. At night, whenever I closed my eyes, I was able to see myself from above, like from a camera in the ceiling. I was both inside my body and outside of it, nearly inseparable from an unknown force trying to control me. I was neither sad nor content. I felt numb for a long time.

It struck me that I had lost my mother to prison and had now lost Rosemary. The old house with its creaky floors and wood-burning fireplace, with its bookshelves and curtains and rugs and antique lamps, was marked with Rosemary's presence. I feared someone else would leave me. I was surprised to feel so afraid. This fear came out of nowhere and left me wondering about life altogether. I feared if I lost control that anyone could leave, including my old friends, my relatives, even Harold and Agnes and George, who had now become a part of me. In a way Rosemary was a part of me. Parts of her are still inside me, and I can feel her there, urging me from time to time.

Even after her death I heard her voice whenever I went to the woods. So each day I went there, where I placed branches and twigs around the spot in the clearing. I arranged them into the shape of a body, a skeleton lying in the dirt. I gathered all the twigs I could, especially the small ones. I twisted them, broke off small pieces, arranged them to create a visual, all bones. I began with a hand, five fingers the length of my own, crooked fingers I rounded at the end with the pocket knife I'd taken from the house. I constructed another hand. By the time it fell dark outside I had arranged an entire body made out of sticks and twigs lying in the dirt. I stepped back and observed it. I stepped to the side and knelt down to get a different angle. I kept looking at it to see what image I could draw from it, maybe the way a sculptor looks at the sculpture, the way a painter looks at color on a canvas.

I imagined with particular clarity how Rosemary sat on the rock with her sketchbook and pulled in one leg, how she let her dark hair fall to one side as she drew. I imagined her back in her bedroom in the house, with the door closed, putting on a black dress and standing in front of the mirror, patting perfume on her neck, glancing at herself. And I imagined myself standing beside her in the image, laughing into her sleeve and then crying and resting my head on her shoulder so that I could smell her fragrance, feel her hand touch my head in comfort. What I loved about the woods was the sense that such images came and went, a new one each day, as if her spirit were there flinging them into me.

All around me were deciduous trees with rough brown trunks, speckled with shadows of strange shapes, the dying grass below almost as brown as the dirt, strewn with rocks and scraps of sunlight slanting in through interlaced branches. I descended the sloping bank toward a stream, where I saw three small deer drinking from the water nearby. They heard the crunching of leaves and looked up at me. I stopped. They watched me, all three of them, as I stood there still, afraid that any movement would cause them to run away in fear. We did this for what seemed like a long time, as I think back, we stared at each other. The moment felt important, as if the woods were trying to tell me something, but I didn't know what was being said. The deer held a skepticism toward me, it was clear. And the moment I took a slow step forward, they turned and scampered away.

George was having considerable trouble handling Rosemary's death. Upstairs in bed, a desk fan whirring on the nightstand beside him, a cold wind howling outside and his body covered in blankets. Even with thunder in the middle of the night, or the windows rattling, or while everyone else was downstairs trying to get on with their lives, George would lie still in his bed. He told me he wanted to lie as still as possible, without blinking, for as long as he could. Time, he said, would move slower so that he wouldn't lose sense of what it felt like to be in the house with Rosemary alive. Harold and Agnes started to worry. I woke up a few nights thinking I felt him touching my brow or kneeling at the foot of my bed. Sometimes he got out of bed and wandered through the house touching the doors, the walls, feeling his way to her.

"It's like I can still feel her spirit in here," he said.

He remembered nothing about his sleepwalking. I saw him walk into the hall in the dark, feeling his way along the wall to her door. I followed him downstairs, where he felt the doorknob of the closet, the front door, and the bathroom. I followed him into the kitchen, where he crawled on his hands and knees to the refrigerator, feeling it with his fingers, whispering to himself. I tried speaking to him, but he didn't respond. He gave an uneasy sigh, which I found exciting in a strange and malicious way. I didn't wake him—I'd always heard you weren't supposed to wake someone during sleepwalking, so I left him there in the dark.

"It's mostly harmless," Agnes told me. "He's never tried to hurt himself or anyone else. As long as he doesn't leave, we'll be fine."

One night he found his way outside into the front yard, in the cold, completely naked. Harold managed to take a blanket and bring him back inside, where he woke disoriented, confused, and sad.

"I feel sad," he told me. "I don't know why. Maybe because Rosemary died."

Strangely, I laughed. It was an uncontrollable reaction, and I could tell it bothered him. This made it worse. I laughed into my shirt. I had to leave the room.

Outside, the weather was getting warmer. The sun was shining more and the trees were turning green. Slowly George felt better. Though I never saw him physically break down and cry, I knew he was sad. Everyone was sad. For several days I continued to go to the woods, feeling numb, yet I couldn't bring myself to feel badly about the way things had turned out, I have to admit. And all this built up. I was already irritable, exhausted.

On a drive out of town to a dental checkup, I asked Liz whether we could stop and visit my mother at the prison, but she said no. She was on a tight schedule, having picked me up early that morning in order to take me to the dentist and return me back to Little Crow so she could still make an important court adjudication hearing that afternoon. The drive was tense and quiet because I had overslept and now I was disappointed, tired, and hungry.

It was ten-thirty in the morning. Liz and I sat in the waiting room at the dentist's office, a room I was familiar with but uncomfortable in every time I visited. The state agency made me go once a year for cleaning and checkups, but my mother had bad teeth and had never enforced good dental hygiene.

"I made a referral to Northside Counseling Services," Liz

told me in the waiting room. "They should be ready to do an intake with us for you in the next few weeks."

"Another counselor," I said.

"They specialize in grief counseling and independent living," she said. "It wouldn't hurt to gain some independent living skills. You'll be sixteen soon."

We were seated in vinyl chairs facing the receptionist area, where two receptionists seemed to be engaged in a deep conversation over a chart on a clipboard one of them held. I recall not feeling well from either allergies or a slight head cold, my nose was stuffy, and I needed a Kleenex, so I went to the desk and one of the receptionists looked at me as if I'd just interrupted something very important. When I asked for a Kleenex she merely pointed to a table with a small box of tissues that I hadn't noticed.

It was this same receptionist who called my name and led me down a hallway to the exam room where I sat in the reclined chair. Her entire face and attitude expressed a revulsion to me. As I think back on it I wonder if she didn't have a child or grandchild who had been burned in some way and looking at my face was a reminder of the terrors of such a thing.

The receptionist told me the hygienist would be in shortly, and I could've sworn she said this while gritting her teeth. She left, closing the door behind her. And there I sat, reclined in the chair, staring around the room, where various posters of decayed teeth and gums lined the walls. There was one framed reproduction of a Norman Rockwell painting, a boy sitting on a barstool at a diner next to a police officer, which struck me as a strange picture to have on the wall with so many photos of teeth and gums.

"Your last visit was over a year ago," the hygienist said when she entered. She tied the paper bib around my neck and reclined my chair all the way. I heard people talking in the hallway, which irritated me. I started to feel angry and I wasn't sure why. The hygienist turned on the lamp above me and asked whether I was brushing my teeth really well and flossing every night.

"Sometimes," I lied.

The hygienist looked at me with her mask covering her mouth. In her hand she held a sharp instrument to scrape my teeth and gums. She told me to open my mouth, and I did, closing my eyes.

"Wider," she said.

I opened wider and she began to scrape my teeth, stabbing my gums, which was painful. She talked to me about brushing as if I'd never done it, emphasizing doing it gently and circular, massaging my gums with the toothbrush. She talked to me about tooth decay.

"Open wide," she said again.

She told me to spit. She leaned back a moment and looked at me behind her mask, telling me about gum disease. She told me about pain and swelling and blood. She stressed flossing, again, all while poking my gums with the sharp instrument.

My head felt light and dizzy. When I spit again and she turned on a slow-speed tool to polish my teeth, I couldn't take any more.

"Open wider," she said, and this time I reached for her wrist. She pulled away, reassuring me the worst was done.

"Stop," I said.

"I'm just polishing," she told me. "It's okay, do you want to hold this? It's harmless. Here." But I didn't want to hold the tool. I felt a fear that grew more intense the longer I heard the whir of the tool in her hand. I reached again for her wrist and gripped it.

"Hey," she said, moving back on her stool and standing. "You just have to cooperate and it'll be over quickly."

"No."

"Sequoyah," she said. "Are you okay?"

My head was aching all of a sudden and I had to close my eyes. I felt light-headed, fatigued, and near panicked by the thought of staying in that room. I wasn't entirely sure why I felt this way—I'd been to the dentist before, but this time felt different. The whole room slanted, and when the hygienist saw how panicked I was she left to get help.

"I don't like it," I said, "I want to leave, I want to go home, do you hear me?"

"What's wrong?" another hygienist said. "What's going on?"

"I don't like it," I said again. I put my hands over my face, sitting up as they started to help me out of the chair. I'm not sure how long I had my hands over my face, but it was long enough for people to come in and out of the room. I heard Liz telling me everything would be all right, and when I removed my hands I saw all of them—Liz, the hygienists, even the surly receptionist with her clipboard, all of them standing there watching me.

"We'll go," Liz said. "It's fine, Sequoyah. We can come back and get your teeth cleaned another time."

WHEN I RETURNED HOME I went upstairs and vomited. It was loud and painful. George was knocking on the door, asking if I was okay, but I ignored him. I'd locked the door and I stayed in there for a long time. Later, I went into my bedroom and pretended to sleep but didn't rest at all. By then the sky had fallen gray, and George's voice trembled as he stood by my bed asking Harold whether I was going to die.

"Of course not," Harold said. "When Agnes gets home we'll call Liz and let her know what's going on. Sound okay, Sequoyah?"

"Fine," I said.

Once Agnes got home and came upstairs, she sat on the edge of the bed and put a cold washcloth on my forehead. She told me about a time when she was a little girl and got lost in a field full of wild brush. She told me about eating muskrat and taking long walks in the country with her mother, who was deaf. Agnes tried to comfort me as best as she could. Then she put her hands on my head and said a prayer that God watch over me and heal any sickness attacking my body. Downstairs, Harold called Liz, who called my doctor who made a referral to a neurological institute. The rest of the night my body was consumed in heat. I shed my clothes and lay sweating on the bed while George snored under his covers all night.

The next day they drove me to Northridge Neurological Institute in Tulsa. They checked me in and a nurse wheeled me down a long hallway to an elevator, which we took up to the seventh floor, then down another long hallway into a room. The window overlooked the post office and downtown buildings. I changed into my gown and got into bed, where they checked my blood pressure, my temperature, and put an IV in my arm to keep me hydrated. My head was hurting and I still felt nauseated.

"How many times have you vomited?" the nurse asked.

"I don't know."

"Several?"

"A bunch."

"And the headaches?"

"He's been having them for several weeks," Harold said.

The nurse typed something in on a computer. "He doesn't have a temperature," she said. "His blood pressure is good. When was the last time you ate anything?"

"He had toast for breakfast," Agnes said. "Nothing else today."

"We'll have to see what the doctor says," she said.

Harold and Agnes followed the nurse out of the room, and

when they returned with a doctor he told me I would stay overnight. He explained that they would be performing an EEG procedure to determine if I was having slight seizures or some sort of neurological disorder. They would study my sleep pattern and my reaction to flashing lights.

"That's all there is to it," the doctor said, and wrote something down on his clipboard. "What you need to try to do is get some rest. A nurse can give you something to help if you're having trouble. A nurse will be back to check on you in a while." He left.

"Seizures?" I said.

"We're worried about your frequent headaches," Harold said. "The procedure isn't bad at all. Just some tests basically. Rosemary had the same thing done last year."

"Everything will be fine," Agnes told me. "We'll leave so you can sleep, and I'll see you tomorrow, okay?"

When I got back into bed I didn't do much except watch TV, some sort of soap opera in Spanish. I thought about Rosemary in the hospital bed, waiting for the same procedure. Rosemary, probably dying for a cigarette. She told me the whole experience was too confining and invasive for her, being observed all night. Every breath monitored, every movement. Some man sitting in a small room, watching her on a screen all night. A machine tracking her brain waves, giving access to some stranger. It was all too much for her. She told me it was like suffocating. But it didn't bother me. I welcomed the idea of being drugged and collapsing into a deep sleep.

I wanted to know what was happening inside my head. Maybe I was morphing into some altered state of consciousness, some other being. I was losing my mind. They would tell me I was part animal, part human, some other entity. I stretched my legs under the covers. I cracked my knuckles and my neck.

When the EEG technologist came in later, she had a small rectangular machine. She told me to sit up and had me look directly into it while a light flashed like a strobe light. It didn't hurt my eyes. She told me to stay relaxed and that I could blink if I needed to. It only took a couple of minutes. Just before she left she told me that once I was asleep she would begin the procedure, basically a sleep study.

"You'll sleep through the whole thing," she said. "Just try to relax."

Soon it was dark outside and I kept watching TV, trying to get comfortable. There was a black-and-white movie on, some gangster movie. A beautiful woman was smoking a cigarette and talking on the phone. She sat with her legs crossed and wore high heels. She was stunning, this woman. I stared at the TV until the nurse came in and interrupted me. She gave me a tiny plastic cup with liquid.

"Drink this," she said. "It'll help you get to sleep."

It was red and sour. She drew the curtains all the way so that it was completely dark except for the light from the TV. I tried to watch the movie, but now there were men in overcoats talking. They kept talking and talking and nothing ever happened. I used the remote to turn the TV off. The medicine eventually kicked in and made me groggy, and I struggled to keep my eyes open. I drifted off to sleep quickly.

I slept a heavy and dreamless sleep. I don't remember anything, not the EEG technologist or a nurse ever being in there. I woke up feeling a pain in my arm from the IV. I saw that a different nurse and the EEG technologist were with me. I vaguely remember hearing their voices, but before I could make out their conversation they saw that I was awake, and the nurse said good morning.

"What time is it?" I asked.

"Quarter till eleven."

"In the morning? I slept that long?"

"I checked on you when I came in to work last night and you were sleeping. You've been asleep the whole time."

The room was bright from the open curtains. I looked at the window and saw that the sun was out. While the EEG technologist wrote something down, the nurse had me sit up so she could change my pillow. "Your days and nights might be mixed up for a couple of days from sleeping so much. That happens to me, too. I work the eleven to eight shift, stay up late and sleep in. That way I can get my shopping done before work if I need to."

"I usually don't sleep well," I said.

"You did last night. Twelve or thirteen hours. You'll sleep well after the doctor prescribes something for you."

I liked the idea of taking sleeping pills. After they left I got my toothbrush out of my bag and brushed my teeth. I wasn't tired at all. I stayed in bed and watched TV most of the morning, flipped through some magazines, then buzzed the nurse and asked for more of the sleep medicine, but they wouldn't give me any more. I closed my eyes, and I must've slept even more because when I opened them I saw Liz and Agnes staring at me. Sunlight flooded the room.

"How are you feeling?" Liz asked, feeling my face like I was sick.

"I'm better," I said.

Harold was sitting in a chair by the window, reading a newspaper. Agnes brought me my clothes, so I went into the bathroom to change. Soon the doctor came in. "Good news," he said, "no signs of epileptic seizures."

"So why the vomiting? He's been sick a lot," Agnes said.

"Has he been through a lot of stress lately?" the doctor asked.

"He's been through a lot," Liz said.

"I don't think he handles stress well, do you, Sequoyah?" Agnes asked.

"Probably high levels of stress," the doctor said, and looked at me. "You need to take it easy, son. Try not to worry so much."

"He's been through a lot," Liz said again.

I was starving, so they took me to eat on the way home. We stopped at a barbecue place off the interstate, and I ordered brisket and ribs. I remember smothering the meat in barbecue sauce and hot sauce and ketchup. I devoured everything, wolfing it down with my hands, eating like an animal. I was so sated in that moment, so freshly and newly awake, I didn't even notice until I got home that all the rooster sauce and ketchup on my shirt looked like blood.

Back home I rested for a few days, sleeping late and watching TV. I started feeling better. George was feeling better, too. Just as easily as he fell into sadness, he came out of it. One evening he began to talk about mountains, snow, and a desire to go places. He spoke of cold places like Mount Kailash in Tibet, the Meili mountain range, Snowbird in Utah, places with giant mountains full of snow. He talked of snow pillows, avalanches, and elevation levels. He talked about precipitation on mountains when winds sweep from the southwest compared to north winds.

"It's all about topography," he told us. "Westerly storms are more perpendicular to the Sierra Nevada than, say, the Central Valley of California."

"What are you talking about?" Harold asked.

"Air."

Harold stared into open space, thinking.

"He's researching snow mountains for school," Agnes said.

"It's about topography," George said again.

We were all in the kitchen for some reason. Agnes put

slivers of parsley and garlic into a pot of boiling water and began peeling a potato. Harold had a Bloody Mary in his hands, which he sipped from.

"Air," George said again, staring at his glass.

The next day I rode along with Agnes as she ran errands, going to the post office, the grocery store, the hardware store. I carried her groceries, pushed the shopping cart, opened the door for her, anything I could do. I felt the need to help her. I even told her I appreciated everything she was doing for me.

"That's really sweet of you to say," she told me.

I never felt guilty about the way things had turned out since I moved in with them. I didn't want them to think anything was my fault. On the drive home I told her about the homeless community by Black River that Rosemary had introduced me to. Agnes didn't know anything about it.

"I'm not surprised Rosemary gave them food," she said. "She had such a giving spirit."

I asked her if we could drive by and see it, but when we got there, all the tents were gone. The trash sacks, all the chairs and firewood—all of it gone.

"They must've moved someplace else," Agnes said.

We drove home, and I felt my sense of attention deepen. I wanted others to have trouble recognizing who I was and what I desired. This was the way a person should live, in obscurity, unrecognized. I thought of my physical body, the burn marks on my face, my long hair, my Cherokee blood. I needed to adapt to my environment, to blend in.

That night George asked me, "What happens when someone close to you dies?"

"I don't know."

"How do people deal with it? Do they die too?"

"Sometimes they do," I said. "Maybe sometimes a part of them dies on the inside. But we can't worry about any of that. I don't want to sit around worrying about people dying."

"I want to figure it out."

"You can't," I told him. "People live and die. Death is quick."

In our room, George and I felt Rosemary's presence between us like a swollen river. It was as if we sensed the pull of some force confirming the uncertainty of life. Nothing would change that.

"I'm reading something to help my inner peace," he said, and began reading to me: "*Alashir's father, a highly intelligent, quiet man, often discussed Christianity and the Ego in great detail with him. One night, after Alashir had returned home, his father peeked in through the bedroom door to watch him perform a meditation and breathing technique—the Bhastrikā, bellows breath (a Hatha Yoga relaxation technique that involves breathing slowly in and out through the nose). His father, who was suspicious of what he saw, fled back downstairs with his asthma inhaler in his mouth with the assumption that Alashir had been brainwashed. Alashir talked about hallucinations, his visions of water and animals, not to mention simple throat and head cleansing—the ujjāyi and kapāla bhāti respectively. Alashir could quote Sanskrit terms and cite whole verses from Sanskrit literature.*"

George looked up at me, waiting for a response.

"I don't know what to say," I said.

"No response?"

"Nothing."

"You'll think about it one day," he said. "Your body and mind will merge. Try to meditate, I think it will help you."

"I don't know," I said. "I don't know what you're talking about. I don't know anything."

"The best thing you can do is empty your mind. Maybe that's the only way to be close to God. Maybe we only have ourselves."

"Rosemary wanted to die," I said. "Nobody did anything wrong. You don't understand. Nobody understands."

"Well, she stole money from Harold. She stole from her work. She stole all the time. I think Harold and Agnes feel terrible about it."

"They do," I said. I started to laugh and couldn't help it. George looked a little afraid.

I went downstairs, where Agnes had fallen asleep in the chair with a magazine on her chest. I saw the light on in the hall leading downstairs to the basement. This had become my routine, checking things before bed. I checked the front door and back door to make sure they were locked. It was a nightly ritual. Not just checking but touching the knobs. In the kitchen I checked the burners on the stove to make sure they were off. I touched the dials, all four of them. I went to the back door and checked it again, touching the knob. Somehow doing the routine made me feel better about going to bed. I'm not sure how it started, or why it started, only that it began sometime after Rosemary died.

I put my hand on Agnes's shoulder and nudged her awake. She opened her eyes and blinked. She squinted at me.

"I must've drifted off," she said.

"I don't know who I am," I told her.

I felt her hand on mine. She looked at me and smiled.

In the weeks that followed I shaved my head into a Mohawk and kept wearing eyeliner, even around the house. For the remainder of the time I stayed with the Troutts, I thought of them as family. Despite everything that had happened, it was better than staying at the shelter, better than any of the other foster families I had stayed with.

As the weather grew warmer, Harold helped me build a tepee in the backyard, where I spent most of my time. George grew more distant and retreated to his typewriter. I started writing my own stories, about Indians and monsters, about brainwashed killers, about mysterious deaths in a mythical Oklahoma town. I mostly kept to myself the rest of my time at the Troutt house. From the tepee I emerged every so often like a horse in the country, like a wavering flame, visible for miles, bracing myself for what was to come.

ACKNOWLEDGMENTS

Many thanks to my family for all their patience and support. Thanks to my editor, Mark Doten, and to Abby Koski, Rachel Kowal, and everyone else at Soho. Thanks to the editors at the Pushcart Prize and to the editors who first published excerpts: Diane Williams and Bradford Morrow—my heroes, both of them. Most of all, a very special thanks to Caroline Eisenmann, my agent, who spent countless hours reading and making suggestions, whose wisdom and guidance helped shape this book to become what it is.

AUTHOR'S NOTE

One of my main concerns when I began writing *Where the Dead Sit Talking* was to illustrate the difficult lives of children who have been in the foster care system, from youth shelters to juvenile detention centers to staying with various foster families. For seven years, from 1999 to 2006, I worked in social services, doing three different jobs, all of which involved working with youth who were on the fringes of collapse, both mentally and physically. I worked with and visited youth who were locked up for committing crimes. I worked with teenagers who were runaways, who were suffering from substance abuse problems, and teenagers who were involved in prostitution and gangs. I worked with teenagers who were shuffled around in the system, moved from foster home to foster home. Many of them simply felt like nobody listened. They felt like nobody cared. Part of Sequoyah's voice grew out of the many voices I heard from youth who were struggling with their emotional pain, with finding their home, and with their identity in terms of both race and gender.

These were difficult jobs I had, and writing about the kind of youth I worked with felt very important to me. I felt they needed a voice, and fiction was one way I could offer a voice for them. The novel is often described as "dark," but there are dark lives all around us. Visit a youth shelter some time. Volunteer to work with what society calls "at-risk" youth, which only provides a negative label and stereotype for teens who are less fortunate than so many others.

Often, I carried what I heard home with me and thought about the struggles so many youth were facing. The advice I was given was to not think about the cases when I left for the day, but how is one supposed to be in a field like social work and not think about the people they're trying to help? How does one talk to a teenager who has tried to commit suicide by swallowing a bottle of pills, been placed in psychiatric care, and then run away in search of a better life—and then not think about it all the time? One thing I saw that the youth I worked with all had in common was that they needed someone to listen to them. They needed to discover who they were and that people accepted them. Sequoyah and Rosemary are both facing the same struggles as the youth I worked with. They want to be accepted, to be liked, to be treated better than their abusers treated them.

An important question I wanted to explore in writing this novel was: What is home? Another important theme I wanted Sequoyah to discover was his search for identity. He wears eyeliner, is half Cherokee, and is facially scarred. He finds

Rosemary so intriguing, in some ways he wants to become her. I often get asked whether I wanted Sequoyah to be seen as dangerous, and the truth is that he is simply broken. He is as broken as the kids I worked with in social services were.

I want to believe the good news is that maybe I made a difference. Maybe I said something to a kid who had given up hope. Maybe today there is another social worker out there working with kids and telling them the things I told them—that the world is full of opportunities and beautiful people and places to see. Many kids often don't realize what the world can offer for them. In *Where the Dead Sit Talking*, Sequoyah, Rosemary, and George are each struggling to understand what the world can offer and how they fit in.

—Brandon Hobson, Oklahoma, 2019

DISCUSSION QUESTIONS

1. Sequoyah is a man looking back on a short period in his life when he was a youth in foster care. How is his voice different than a fifteen-year-old telling the story? What details does he add or leave out that a teenager might tell differently?

2. How does Sequoyah's difficult home life affect his relationships with the people he meets?

3. Sequoyah says he would like to be Rosemary and even finds himself sneaking into her room and into her closet to explore. What feelings do you think he is experiencing regarding his own gender or identity?

4. Is Sequoyah a reliable narrator? Why or why not?

5. Does Sequoyah seem dangerous? Why is George afraid of him?

6. How are George and Sequoyah alike as fostered youth? How are they different?

7. In what ways are the Troutts effective (or not effective) foster parents?

8. What role does Sequoyah play in what ultimately happens to Rosemary?

9. How does Sequoyah change from the beginning of the book to the end?

10. How does displacement serve as a central theme to the book? Do foster children like Sequoyah mirror the way Cherokees and other tribes were forced out of their land in the late 1800s before walking the Trail of Tears?

ABOUT THE AUTHOR

Brandon Hobson's most recent novel, *Where the Dead Sit Talking*, was a finalist for the 2018 National Book Award, longlisted for the 2019 Aspen Words Literary Prize, and won the In the Margins Book Award. He is the author of three previous works of fiction: *Desolation of Avenues Untold*, *Deep Ellum*, and *The Levitationist*. He has received a Pushcart Prize, and his stories and essays have appeared in such places as *The Believer*, *Conjunctions*, *NOON*, The Paris Review Daily, *Publishers Weekly*, and elsewhere. Before completing a PhD in Creative Writing from Oklahoma State University, he was for seven years a social worker who worked with youths labeled "at risk." Beginning Fall 2019 he will be an Assistant Professor of Creative Writing at New Mexico State University. Hobson is an enrolled citizen of the Cherokee Nation Tribe of Oklahoma.